Bamfords Shroud

by

HAROLD NICHOLSON

HORSESHOE PUBLICATIONS • WARRINGTON • CHESHIRE

First published 1999

ISBN 1.899310.09.6

British Library Cataloguing in Publication Data.
A Catalogue record for this book is available from the British Library.

Printed and bound in Great Britain by
PRINT EXPRESS SERVICES LTD.
Frodsham,
Cheshire WA6 7HL

for the Publishers
HORSESHOE PUBLICATIONS
Box 37, Kingsley, Warrington
Cheshire WA6 8DR

Cover designed and illustrated by PETER NICHOLSON.

Bamfords Shroud

A beautiful blonde-haired woman.

The woman of your dreams, but are they dreams, or is she an evil illusion?

Ralph Grant, ex-officer, late of the Scottish Highlanders regiment finds himself ensnared in a web of fantasy and terror, the unexplained and evil incarnate.

He meets his true love and the portly Inspector Sharp who against all his instincts and training gives credence to Ralph's story.

CHAPTER ONE

What I am about to tell you, you may or may not believe. But I shall tell it to you as it was told to me by an old and trusted friend who swore on the Bible that every word was true.

It all started one day late in September in the year 1918. A young ex-officer, late of the Scottish Highlanders, boarded a train at Exeter for the North. His name was Ralph Grant. He was a good six feet tall and slim. His good looks, that had made many a young girl's heart flutter, had gone. The great battle of the Somme in 1916 had left him disfigured. Scars covered the left side of his face, leaving him very self-conscious. The hair that was once blond was now white, the constant shelling had seen to that. Bright blue eyes that were once full of laughter were now forever watchful for other eyes that would stare at him.

Ralph had just spent two years in a sanatorium recovering not only from his multiple burns but also from the scars that were left on his mind. During his stay there he had met and made friends with a Major Jack Ryan. The Major had lost both legs in the last great battle at Ypres and had only been at the sanatorium a few months but they had taken to each other like long-lost brothers. Major Jack owned a cottage in the Lake District and had promised Ralph an unlimited stay there.

"You take the place for as long as you like, old chap," he had said. "It's no damned good to me now. I've no legs for gadding about the countryside."

Major Ryan had died one month earlier but his wife, who Ralph had never met, had kept to her husband's promise. Everything had been arranged for him a first class rail ticket and transport to the cottage when he arrived.

The porter had settled him into his reserved seat next to the window. The station was crowded mainly by soldiers saying their good-byes to sweet-hearts, family or friends and he wished them well wherever they were bound. Soon the train began to move, pulling and tugging as it strove to take its charges to their various destinations. There were shouts of "good-bye" and "don't forget to write" mixed with the smoke and steam that enveloped the platform.

Ralph felt pleased that no-one else had endeavoured to share his compartment. He would have peace and quiet all the way to Crewe. There would be plenty of time to read and wallow in his thoughts. Thoughts of what he would do when he arrived at the cottage. There would be fishing: oh, he hadn't fished for years . The last time had been with his father.

"Now where was it?" He thought as his mind went back to the days before the war.

"Oh, I remember, it was the Kyle of Tongue. We hired a small boat."

Then he smiled as he recalled the good times he had shared with his father.

His mother had died many years before the war when he was just ten years old; his father only twelve months ago. The death of his father had come as a great shock to him and had set him back many months from his recovery. But now he felt fine, he had put everything behind him and was looking forward to doing just what he liked. It was going to be wonderful.

Ralph flicked through the assortment of magazines that he had quickly purchased at the news stand on the station platform. As he browsed through one called 'The Theatre' he came across a photograph of a young woman. She instantly reminded him of a French girl that he had met while on leave in Paris. She too had long flowing hair, the colour of ripening corn with the sun shining on it.

He put the magazine down beside him and gazed out of the window. But he wasn't seeing anything. In his mind he was walking along the banks of the Seine hand in hand with his Mimi.

"God, she was beautiful!" he said to himself as he remembered the wonderful never to be forgotten two weeks that they had shared. The music, the opera, dancing at the Cafe Royal and the exotic nights he had spent in her arms. He knew that she was a prostitute and that he would never see her again, but he would never ever forget her.

He had never been with a woman since. The Somme had seen to that. And he put his hand up to his face as a voice cried from his soul.

"Why have there got to be wars? Why can't everything be as it was in Paris?"

After a period of reading he felt tired. So it wasn't long before the rocking of the train and the rhythmic sound of the wheels playing over the tracks lulled him into a deep sleep. But with sleep came the horrible nightmares: battles raging, shells bursting, screams of men in terrible pain.

He was once again shouting orders, then there was whistling in his mixed-up turmoil and he awoke shouting: "Over the top, lads."

He was standing in the compartment with his arm raised high, sweat pouring from him, when he realised where he was. Someone was shouting something and he could hear a whistle blowing. There were people walking past the window.

"Crewe! Crewe Station."

A porter shouted as he opened the carriage doors.

Ralph, who was still in semi-shock over his dream, reached for his small case from the luggage rack as the door opened.

"Crewe Junction, sir" said the porter. "All change here."

"Keswick! I'm going to Keswick," Ralph blurted out, still a bit flustered.

The porter looked at him and smiled. He could see that something was wrong and couldn't help but see the scars on the passenger's face. He immediately took charge of the situation.

"Keswick is it, sir? Lovely place, Keswick. I went there before the war. Now, sir, have you any more luggage besides this?"

He carried on taking the case from Ralph.

"A trunk in the guard's van," replied Ralph.

"Your name, sir?" asked the porter.

"Grant," answered Ralph, getting down onto the platform.

"You leave everything to me, sir," the porter said, following him.

Crewe Junction was crammed with people. There seemed to be soldiers from all parts of the British Empire and even some Americans: it was Bedlam. It seemed like a miracle to Ralph that the porter managed to get him and his trunk safely aboard the train to Penrith. But two hours later, and after several stops in the black industrial north with its factory chimneys belching out clouds of smoke, he was being enthralled by beautiful scenery.

Autumn had come early to Shap Fell. Glorious reds, delicate yellows and majestic rusts covered the landscape, giving a warning of an early winter. The sturdy farmhouses built of local stone reminded him of the crofters' cottages in Scotland. Herds of sheep were taking the last remaining morsels of nourishment before the snows came. Penrith station seemed a far cry from Crewe. The ancient capital of Cumberland with its great historic past seemed to welcome him with peace and quiet. As he stood there drinking in the afternoon sunshine the local train to Keswick came puffing along the track.

“What a change from the other trains,” he thought. “It could be a cousin of the Rocket with that tall smoke-stack.”

The little train soon began showing its paces as it tugged the two coaches up towards Keswick. It wasn’t long before he was looking up at the towering bulks of Skiddaw and Saddleback. Ralph felt an inner glow as he contemplated his stay at the cottage.

“This is going to be the holiday of a lifetime,” he thought. “No wonder great poets like Wordsworth, Tennyson and Shelley came to love the place!”

He was soon brought back to reality when the little train pulled its way into Keswick station. It was now late afternoon and the sun was starting to dip behind Grisedale Pike. Ralph was supervising the unloading of his trunk when a porter approached him and asked “Are you Mr Grant, sir?”

Ralph said that he was.

“There’s someone waiting for you, sir,” the man carried on. “A chap with a horse and trap. Says he’s to take you to some cottage or other.”

“Oh good, he’s here, then,” replied Ralph. Then as an afterthought: “A horse and trap, eh! That should be pleasant.”

The porter looked at him as though he was mad and retorted: “I wouldn’t be very happy taking a ride with that one if I was you.”

He looked round to see if anyone was listening and came closer to Ralph, whispering: “I’d be careful if I was you, sir. I know everyone hereabouts but I’ve never set eyes on that one before. He looks a rum ‘un if you ask me.”

Ralph smiled and didn’t take much notice of the porter, who went away shaking his head. The driver and his horse and trap were waiting outside the station.

Ralph tried to make conversation with him. “How far was the cottage? Would it take long to get there?”

But the driver just sat looking ahead and did not answer.

As soon as Ralph and his trunk were on the trap the man cracked his whip at the black stallion in the shafts. Suddenly without warning the horse set off, throwing Ralph to the floor of the trap.

“Hold on there!” he shouted at the driver. “Slow down, can’t you?”

For the first time the driver looked round at him. Ralph was trying to get to his seat but when he saw the man’s face he fell back onto the floor in horror. The driver laughed a horrible laugh, showing a mouth full of rotten teeth. His face was even more disfigured than Ralph's own. The whole left-hand side hung in folds as though he'd had a stroke. The left eye was lower than the right one and they both seemed to glow in the evening gloom. He laughed louder and the black stallion seemed to answer him with an even louder neigh.

After many attempts Ralph managed to get to his seat. He knew now what the porter meant and as he clung on for dear life he kept his eyes firmly fixed on the driver.

As night closed in and darkness fell he lost his bearings. All that he knew was that they were going up into the hills. He could see lights from the dwellings down below. Suddenly they were surrounded by trees and the night seemed even darker as clouds covered the moon and stars.

Spots of rain began to fall. It was the start of an overture for the storm that was about to hit them. A gale force wind sprang from nowhere sending the trees wildly thrashing their branches at the torrential rain that poured down on them.

Ralph was soaked to the skin. The trap was awash with rain filling his shoes as it slopped from side to side. Then a tremendous flash of lightning split the black sky followed by a monumental clap of thunder. The stallion reared in panic and raced off at break-neck speed along the rough track. Ralph clung on even tighter. The driver, who was enjoying every minute, stood up and cracked his whip at the stallion, roaring with laughter as he did so. Thunder and lightning seemed to be coming from all sides. Ralph clapped his hands over his ears. It was frightening, horrific: it was France all over again and he slumped to the bottom of the trap as he had done in many a shell hole.

They must have travelled miles or it seemed that to Ralph when they finally stopped. The storm was still raging as Ralph dragged himself to an upright position and looked about him. The driver never moved. The black stallion snorted as it scraped its hooves nervously. Ralph stood up and opening the little door at the back of the trap he stepped down on to the muddy road. Still the driver didn't move. Ralph looked around for some sign of where they were but all was in darkness. The rain was coming down in torrents. Suddenly the driver turned, picked up the trunk as though it were a hat-box and threw it onto the muddy track, making a snarling noise as he did so. The whip cracked again and he laughed hideously as he raced off into the stormy night.

Ralph looked around in desperation.

"Where the hell am I?" he shouted after the driver.

It was then that a flash of lightning lit up his surroundings and in the light he saw the cottage. It was about thirty yards away to his right.

"Thank God for that," he thought as he started to drag his trunk through the mud.

He finally arrived at the cottage door covered in mud and gasping for breath after slipping over three times.

"I hope this bloody door's open," he said as he felt for the latch in the dark. "That fool of a driver never gave me a key."

At last something was going his way. The latch was found and the door swung open. He dragged the trunk inside and slammed the door shut against the storm. But his troubles hadn't finished. It was pitch black and he couldn't see a thing.

"Damn it!" he swore as he banged his shin on the trunk. He fumbled in his inside pocket trying to find his matches which he had wrapped in grease proof paper. It was a habit he had picked up in the trenches. Drawing them out triumphantly he unwrapped the paper and took hold of the silver match box that his father had given to him when he embarked for France. Slowly he opened the lid and carefully took out a match.

"My God, I hope they're not damp," he muttered as he struck the match against the rough edge of the box. Once, twice and then the third time of striking there was a spark and the match blazed into life, showing him that he was in a small entrance hall with a door to the right.

He quickly went across and opened it. But as he did so a strong draught blew from the room making him turn away and blowing out the match. When he turned around he couldn't believe his eyes. The room was aglow with candles. There was a good fire burning in the fireplace.

Ralph peeped in, fully expecting someone to be there and called "Hello! Anyone there?"

His call was greeted by silence.

"Hello!" he called again, as he walked around.

Still no reply. He couldn't understand it. The place looked lived in. It was as though someone had just nipped out. There was a good spread on the table, ham, cheese, bread, fruit and a jug of ale.

He opened one of the two remaining doors and called again before he passed through it. Still all was silent.

He had entered a small bedroom that was mainly filled by a double bed. Retracing his steps he tried the other door. He found himself looking into the black night and the storm. He quickly closed it and returned to the main room and the warming fire.

"This is all very strange!" he thought as he seated himself in the only chair, tugging at his sodden shoes. "I must be in the right place."

An hour later he had dried himself and changed into his night attire.

After throwing a couple of logs that were stacked by the fire-place onto the fire he sat down and began to eat of the fare from the table. Ralph looked around, taking in his surroundings. The room felt cosy and it made him feel at home. The half dozen candles that flickered about the room projected strange shadows on the ceiling, making the large oak beams appear even larger. The floor consisted of stone flags and the walls of grey local stone. He considered that the whole cottage must have been built from materials found in and around the district.

"Yes, I'm going to enjoy it here," he said out loud as he stretched to the full.

He was feeling tired and gave out a loud yawn. But as he sat there he began to think of the strange man on the trap and the stranger things that had happened since his arrival, the candles, the fire being lit, the food on the table...Who had done it? And where were they now? Whoever they were, he was grateful and he snuggled deeper into his dressing-gown as the storm beat against the windows.

It wasn't long before he was fast asleep. The day's events had left him exhausted, but this sleep was a wonderful sleep. There were no nightmares as before. Gone were the shells and the screams of wounded. All was peace and tranquillity. He dreamt that he was beside a lake. The water was smooth like glass and gentle ripples lapped around his feet. Then a mist arose from the centre of the lake and came towards him. Out of the mist a small rowing boat glided ever nearer. Standing in the boat was a beautiful woman dressed in a white silk gown. She had long flowing yellow hair and as she came nearer she called to him. His heart beat faster. It was his Mimi. His Mimi had come to him across the water. Soon they were in each other's arms kissing and laughing as they danced together along the lake's edge.

The next thing he knew they were in a bedroom. There was champagne and more dancing more laughter. Mimi was taking off her gown and she stood before him in all her beauty. Then she started to dance around him in an exotic breathtaking fashion. The more she danced the more he wanted her, and in his sleep he cried out for her to come to him. The mist came again and covered the bed. Then she came to him, gliding through the mist as she had done on the lake, and he was in paradise.

In his wonderful dream she stayed with him all night. But somewhere deep down in his subconscious mind, a voice was calling to him: "Beware, beware: all is not what it seems."

The next morning he awoke slowly. In his drowsy state he remembered his dream and smiled. A warm glow came over him as he recalled every detail as though it were real and had actually happened.

Suddenly he sat up and looked around him. He was in the double bed. Naked in the double bed.

"What the hell am I doing here?" he whispered. "How did I get here? I remember dozing in the chair."

Then he stopped short as he saw his night clothes scattered around the floor and a champagne bottle with two glasses lying with them.

"My God!" he cried as he leapt out of bed and picked up the bottle.

"It really did happen, Mimi must be here!"

He rushed to the door snatching up his dressing gown and slipping it over his naked body.

He entered the main room excited and fully expecting Mimi to be there. But the room was quiet except for the sizzling of bacon in a large frying pan that stood on a griddle over the fire.

He went over to it and as the aroma of the frying feast touched his nostrils, he cried "She's here, she's here!" and he rushed outside like an excited schoolboy, shouting her name.

The wind was still blowing and there were a few spots of rain falling, but he didn't care about that.

"Mimi!" he called "Mimi!"

He dashed around the mud-sodden ground in his bare feet but there was no response to his calls except from a solitary crow who screeched a reply from a nearby tree.

Dejected and bewildered he went back into the cottage. It was the smell of burning bacon that brought him back to reality and he dashed over to the fire, just managing to save the remnants of his breakfast.

"What's going on?" he cried in desperation as he slumped into the arm-chair. "What the hell is happening to me?"

He leant forward, dropping his head into his upturned hands.

He stood up and shouted at the empty room.

"It's driving me mad! Do you hear, whoever you are? Mad!"

CHAPTER TWO

In the afternoon of the first day he went for a walk. Trying to find his bearings was the initial cause for the expedition, but trying to clear his mind and put things into perspective was uppermost in his thoughts. Wearing his Harris Tweed suit and cap and slipping into his old army trench coat along with a stout pair of boots, he was well insulated against anything the weather could throw at him. But as he walked further away from the cottage he found himself looking back. Something was telling him not to go too far. He had a strong feeling of fear that he might get lost and at the back of his mind he still believed that Mimi had been with him the night before. It was all too real for him to believe anything else. He was a rational man, so it couldn't be anything else.

He had climbed high up a nearby hill and as he leaned over a stone wall he could see a lake. But he didn't know which one. Was it Derwentwater, Bassenthwaite Lake or Thirlmere?

Suddenly he had an overpowering feeling that he had to get back to the cottage and he turned in panic, slipping and sliding down the hill in his haste to get there. The feeling was that she would be waiting for him, waiting there with her arms wide open, longing to hold him in her warm embrace. The feeling was so strong that he ran the last hundred yards to the cottage door.

Bursting it open he shouted her name. Time and again he shouted as he blundered in and around the cottage. But yet again there was no sight of her and once again he was in deep despair as he collapsed inconsolable onto the bed.

The walk, the climb up the hill and the strenuous run back to the cottage, only to be filled with dismay at the outcome, had been too much for him and he drifted off into a deep sleep.

As he slept the dream came again, bringing his Mimi back to him. His desire for her knew no bounds, but the voice within him cried out "beware."

The next day was the same and the next, until, after a week of untold rapture in his dreams, he was going crazy for her. He wouldn't eat, he hardly went out of the cottage and each day the voice inside him called for him to beware. Each day it grew louder and louder until by the end of the week it was screaming inside his head.

On the eighth night he went to bed early hoping she would come to him quickly and put him out of his misery. But it was not to be, for as he slept the nightmares returned.

And so it was for four nights and four days. Mimi had abandoned him.

He hadn't eaten for days and he was frightened to go to sleep, not knowing what would happen. The food had all gone and what had been left was eaten by marauding mice who had invaded the cottage. The cottage changed. Cobwebs hung everywhere. The fire wouldn't light. When he tried to light it, smoke filled the room. The whole place seemed to be falling into disrepair. There were great holes in the roof that let the rain pour in and so in desperation he left, looking more like a tramp than the fine figure of a young officer that had arrived there twelve days before.

Haggard, dirty and un-shaven Ralph wandered off, not knowing where or in which direction. He wandered for miles, his body giving in for lack of nourishment.

It was raining but his mind knew nothing of that. Staggering and falling he finally collapsed and passed out. It was early evening when he opened his eyes. Strangely enough he felt well and relaxed. His mind was alert and he was himself again. He could think clearly and rationally and all that had passed was clear in his mind. He remembered everything.

"How could it happen?" he thought, as he sat there beneath a tree.

The rain had stopped and he was in a wood. Where, he didn't know and he didn't seem to care. His spirits were high and getting higher. Suddenly he started to laugh, at what he didn't know, but it felt good.

Standing up, he brushed himself down. His clothes were wet and his bones were stiff.

"Just like being in France," he said, laughing, as he set off again.

"Now what I want is some food and a wash. A good razor and soap wouldn't come amiss either," he thought, rubbing his chin.

He hadn't gone far when he heard someone laughing. It sounded like children. Ralph stopped short, trying to figure out from which direction the sound was coming.

"God, somebody human at last," he thought. "They'll be able to tell me where I am," and he set off in the direction of the laugher.

About fifty yards on he saw some figures running about between the trees. As he came closer he could see them clearly and he froze to the spot. For there in front of him was a woman with long blonde hair, wearing a long white dress. She was playing with a young girl. They were chasing each other through the deep autumn leaves.

"My God, it's her!" he gasped as his heart missed a beat.

The woman looked up at the sky and called to the girl that it was time to go The young girl answered, calling her "My Lady."

Ralph looked puzzled at this remark and on closer inspection of the woman he realised that it wasn't Mimi at all. Doubt entered his mind as he recalled the voice that screamed from within, telling him to beware.

But he also remembered his glorious nights of passion and if it wasn't Mimi but this woman, then he wanted to know her more than anything in the world.

Instead of approaching them he decided to follow and discover where she lived and who she was. He would solve once and for all the mystery of the cottage and maybe find the woman of his dreams.

The woman and the young girl moved off through the trees, skipping and laughing as they went. Ralph followed not too far behind, keeping well hidden amongst the trees. Soon they came to the edge of the wood and began to climb up a steep hill. Ralph let them reach the top before emerging from the wood. Then as they passed over the summit he climbed as fast as he could to catch up with them. But as he too reached the summit he found to his dismay that they had disappeared into a mist at the bottom of the next valley.

"Damn and blast it!" he swore.

"What do I do now? Which way did they go?" he said, looking about him.

"They must have gone into that mist. There's nowhere else they could have gone." He set off down into the valley heading for he didn't know what.

As he entered the mist he found that he could only see a few feet either way and he had to tread carefully. The mist was so thick that he didn't know whether he was going straight or around in circles.

"Damn this fog," he said as he stumbled along. "When is it going to end?"

Just as he had spoken the mist started to thin out and he found himself near to a path that led down the valley. It was getting quite dark but the sky was clear and the first stars were out as he quickened his step. He could just see a clump of trees ahead of him, and as he came to them a light then another and another.

"It's a village!" he cried, overjoyed at the sight of civilisation. "Thank God for that," and he set off with renewed vigour.

It was a small village. Just one road with a few houses on either side. He noticed that they were old-fashioned houses. Some were Tudor, some had thatched roofs. There were lights in some of the windows and a dog barked in the distance. He felt at home in these pleasant surroundings.

Nestled to one side in the centre of the village he came across the village inn.

"This is what I want," he said looking up at the sign and reading it out loud: "The Manor House." With a thirst and hunger enough for three men he opened the door and entered.

The inn like the rest of the village was old. In fact he had never seen such an establishment. The bar was a long trestle table. There were no beer pumps and the customers, although the place was empty at the moment, must have been served from large stone jugs that stood in front of three huge barrels that rested on a cradle behind the bar. The room was small and Ralph's head nearly touched the oak beams that supported the low ceiling. The walls, like the ceiling, were made of beams and plaster. All but the fireplace rang true of Tudor style. It was made of local grey stone and he wondered why a Tudor village in all its glory was nestling snug in a Lake District valley.

"Hello! Is anyone there?" he called and waited for a reply.

"Hello!" he called again.

There was a noise in the back and soon a small man came in and seemed very surprised to see him.

"Yes, sir?" he said. "What can I do for you?."

The little man, who was thin and balding, looked about him as though something was wrong. His shifty eyes were everywhere. He was like a rat trapped in a corner. Ralph glanced around to see what he was looking at.

"I'd like a drink and something to eat, if you please," said Ralph, going nearer to the bar and into the glow of a solitary candle.

As he approached the little man's eyes opened wide with horror as he stared at Ralph's face. He took a pace backwards and called to someone at the back.

"Go and get the father, Father Ross! Get Father Ross!" and he held out his arm towards Ralph shouting "Don't come near me. Keep away."

"What's wrong?" Ralph asked, getting closer. "What have I done?"

"I said keep away from me," screamed the little man "You have the mark of the Devil on your face."

“The mark of the Devil?” laughed Ralph. “This was done in the War.”

“Aha!” shouted the little man “There hasn’t been a war for years. That is the mark of the Devil. She has sent you here. You are one of her conquests and now one of her disciples.”

“What are you talking about, you stupid man?” said Ralph, getting angry. “Who the hell...?”

“Yes, hell!” shouted the little man jumping up and down. “You know all about hell, don’t you? You and her.”

Ralph was getting wild and was just going to grab the frightened little man when a voice from behind him said:

“Don’t strike him, my son, he knows no better.”

Ralph spun around and there standing in the gloom was a priest.

He was similar in build to Ralph and his hair was white but long, reaching past his shoulders. His face was pale and thin, making his sharp features look even sharper.

“Good evening, Father,” Ralph said, holding out his hand.

“Would you tell this idiot that this is not the mark of the Devil!” he added, touching his face.

The priest smiled and came over to Ralph to shake his hand.

“It’s not the mark of the Devil, Joss, it’s a wound or a fire burn. This poor man is not one of hers,” the priest called to the frightened man.

The little man didn’t seem so sure and still kept his distance.

“All I want is food and drink,” Ralph said to the priest. “By the way, my name is Ralph Grant.”

“I am Father Ross, my son,” the priest replied. “Come with me. I will give you food and shelter.”

Then turning to the still frightened Joss he said “It’s the Lord’s work, Joss. The Lord has sent him to us. He will be safe now.” With that he led Ralph out of the inn and down the village street.

Outside the wind had got up and it had started to rain heavily. The priest grabbed Ralph by the arm and called to him “Hurry, this is no place to be after dark. Evil abounds here,” and he rushed off, pulling Ralph behind him.

Ralph didn't argue. He had seen enough on his short stay to last him a lifetime and he didn't need the priest to help him along.

The rain was turning to sleet and the wind blew stronger as they reached a lychgate that led into a church yard. Ralph had seen enough of the storms in the area to know that this one was bad. They had to use all their strength against the wind.

"Not far now," Father Ross shouted over the howling of the wind.

The trees in the graveyard thrashed their branches at them as they passed between the gravestones. Father Ross, his white hair streaming behind him, made a spectacular figure as he led the way.

Behind the gravestones stood a small Norman church and as they went by the wind was ringing the bell in the tower. A little further on they came to an old stone house that was built more like a fortress.

Father Ross led the way up a flight of stone steps to a strong oak door. He swung on a large handle and gave a mighty push. The heavy door swung open.

"Come in, Master Grant, come in!" cried the priest as he slammed the door shut with the aid of Ralph.

"Stand a moment while I light a candle to show the way," the priest said, fumbling in the dark.

Ralph stood waiting. Then from out of the darkness a spark, then another and another were followed by the priest blowing, suddenly a flame sprang to life and the priest gave a sound of satisfaction.

"Well I never," thought Ralph. "A tinder box!"

When the candles were lit Ralph could see that he was standing in a fine hall that had a grand oak staircase rising from the centre. There were several doors leading off to other rooms and Father Ross led him to one.

"Here we are, Master Grant," the priest said, setting the candlestick down on a large table. "We shall soon have a fire and a glass of brandy to warm us up."

He went over to the wide open fire-place to rouse the dying embers, leaving Ralph to look around the room.

It was sparsely furnished: a sideboard-cum-bookcase stood against one wall, the books were few and far between, three tall ladder-back chairs were near to the table, and two large winged chairs were placed either side of the fireplace.

The fire was springing back to life and the priest added a few more logs to feed it. Ralph moved nearer the blaze.

"That's it, Master Grant," the priest said, holding out his hand and showing Ralph a chair by the fire. "Sit down and get warm. Take the chill from your bones and I will get the brandy to help it."

He went across to the sideboard, bringing back a bottle and two glasses.

All this time Ralph did not utter a word. He felt tired and was content to watch the priest going about his tasks. but his mind was troubled. There were lots of things he wanted to know.

"What was all this 'Devil' nonsense the man at the inn babbled about?" he thought. "And who was this 'she' they kept talking of? There 'hadn't been a war for years', where the hell had they been? The village, the inn, this place and a tinder-box. In this day and age! I know things are backward in the country but things here are ancient."

The priest spoke again.

"It is very pleasant to have a new face in this house, Master Grant. 'Tis a long time since I entertained a gentleman with a glass of brandy."

Ralph smiled and nodded as the priest carried on.

"How did you come by our village, young sir?" he asked.

Ralph thought for a moment before replying.

"I was following someone and became lost in the mist," he said. "The next thing I knew I was here."

"You were very fortunate, my son. Many people have been lost in the mist never to be found again," the priest replied.

There was a lull in the conversation as they both stared into the fire. It was Ralph who spoke first, he couldn't contain his questions any longer.

"Father Ross" he started. "I don't want to sound ungrateful but what was all that about 'Devil marks' back at the inn? That man was really frightened of me."

The priest looked at him and smiled as he nodded his head.

"I knew it had to come," he said. "I have been waiting for your questions, my son. A man of your intelligence will want to know. I suppose that you have noticed other things that demand answers too. It is a sad and terrifying tale of my village and the people who live here."

Then his story began.

"Out there in the mist was a fine manor house and the squire who lived there owned all the land for miles around. He was an old man, kind and generous to all his people. It was in the reign of Charles I and a few years before the Civil War. The old man went to London and was duped by the king into marrying a young wife forty years his junior. It was a disaster from the start. Sir James Bamford was the squire and his wife the Lady Mary.

"It wasn't long before things started to go wrong. He was too old for her bed and she was beautiful and young, but wicked. She had come from a decadent society at the king's court, being used to gay times and the attention of many young men. Here in this wilderness she soon became bored and turned to mischief. Many young men were flattered that this beautiful worldly temptress with her long fair hair would bless them with her favours."

"In one year after her arrival in these parts three young men were dead."

"They had taken their own lives. Four left the district never to be seen again. Nearly every family in the village had been touched by her wickedness."

"The old squire died of shame, so it is said, leaving her to do just as she pleased. It wasn't enough for her to have wild parties at the Manor. She turned her wicked ways to the Devil and witchcraft. Children went missing, graves were defiled, people died of mysterious ailments. Anyone that wouldn't do her bidding disappeared or was found dead."

"Why didn't the people leave?" Ralph interrupted.

"Where would they go?" replied Father Ross. "The Civil War was about to commence and we hoped that Cromwell and his Ironsides would put a stop to it, but it was not to be. It was five years of misery, death, pox, every evil thing that you could think of was heaped upon us."

"Our saviour, as we thought, came in the form of Jacob Clegg the witch finder. The villagers were jubilant and marched on the Manor, dragging her out. She was put on trial in her own house and sentenced to death by burning at the stake. She laid down curses at her trial. Curses on us all and our children. She swore on the Devil that she would return and pursue her vengeance until the end of time."

He stopped and buried his head in his hands.

Ralph didn't know what to say. What he had heard had solved the mystery of the cottage and it made his blood run cold. It was not Mimi as he had thought, but this Lady Mary Bamford who had shared his dreams.

"What happened next?" asked Ralph, determined to hear the whole story. The priest sat up and took a sip of his brandy.

"It was about one month after the burning that a villager came screaming into the inn swearing that he had seen her at the Manor House.

The villagers didn't laugh at him. They took it seriously, for they believed that she had come back to fulfil her curses

"They came to me."

At this point Ralph looked flabbergasted and blurted out.

"Came to you? Are you trying to tell me that you and all these people are the same people that lived here nearly three hundred years ago?."

Father Ross looked at Ralph and the pain in his eyes was enough to convince Ralph that he was telling the unbelievable truth.

"My God!" gasped Ralph. "But how?"

"I persuaded them that the only way to get rid of her was to burn down the Manor House. Then her spirit would have nowhere to go."

Suddenly Father Ross jumped up, giving Ralph a fright, and began to suffer an inner agony, reaching out as though talking to God.

"Why did they listen to me?" he cried. "What have we done to deserve this everlasting torment?"

Ralph stood up and putting his arm around the priest led him back to his seat.

It was quite some time before Father Ross regained his composure.

After another brandy he carried on.

"Early one morning we set off with cart-loads of wood, determined to end it once and for all. When we arrived the place was empty. It had been stripped bare by Cromwell's men. We piled wood in every room and set fire to it. Soon the whole Manor House was ablaze from end to end. Smoke filled the morning sky. Suddenly there was a shout and everyone looked to the roof. There she was, arms out-stretched, laughing at us.

"As she waved her arms first one way then another the smoke drifted high into the hills, encircling the whole valley. Then she disappeared. We thought that we had won and we celebrated the rest of the day."

"The next morning the villagers awoke feeling the worst for the drink and found that the smoke had turned into a mist. Six of them went up to investigate but only one returned. He was raving mad and died two days later."

"No-one left the valley for eight months. The villagers noticed that the children weren't growing. They didn't seem to be in any harm. They just stayed the way they were. We thought that this must be the curse that she had put on us. It was exactly one year to the day of the burning that she appeared again and it was I who saw her."

"I pleaded with her to set the children free but she poured scorn on my request. And then she told me to my horror that it wasn't only the children for whom time had stood still, but all that lived in the valley. And from that day you see us as we were two hundred and eighty five years ago."

"That is incredible!" said Ralph softly. "But why haven't people come here? Somebody must have tried to find out what had happened!"

"Oh yes," laughed the priest nervously. "People have come here: people like you. I have a graveyard full of them. All of them young men. Each one had been seduced by that she-Devil, their bodies and minds broken. They were led here to die."

Ralph's mouth dropped open when he realised the priest knew that he too had been involved with Lady Mary Bamford. Father Ross carried on.

"You see, my son, this sort of thing has been happening ever since the mist arrived. She has no use for us in the village. She has to get her victims from outside and when she has had her pleasure ..."

Ralph cut him short.

"My God!" he blurted, "That's what she's done to me. She's brought me here to die!"

Panic set in as he cried out "What am I going to do?."

Father Ross came across to him and gripped him on his shoulders.

"Fear not, Master Grant," he cried and he seemed almost happy . "You shall not die. As I said to Joss at the inn, you have been sent to us. You are our salvation."

Ralph calmed down when he heard this but he couldn't understand what the priest meant and it showed on his face.

"You see, my son," the priest carried on. "You are the first one to come to us fit and well. You are not mad. You have known her but she couldn't destroy you. You have won a famous victory!"

He clasped his hands together as though in prayer and said: "Praise be to God for this sign of deliverance."

Ralph was still not convinced and couldn't share the priest's exuberance.

"She'll know I'm still alive," he replied angrily. "She could come for me at anytime. Then what am I supposed to do?"

"Don't get alarmed, my son," Father Ross said calmly. "I can protect you against her. If you do as I say, she will not hurt you any more."

Ralph sank back into the big chair, still not convinced by the priest's argument.

"How does he know what I've been through?" he thought. "How can he protect me against a thing that comes to me in my dreams, a thing that can drive you mad? Here he is telling me not to worry and he's got a graveyard full of bodies out there that she has killed. God, what a situation to be in!"

All this time Father Ross had been rummaging through a cupboard in the large sideboard.

"Ah, here we are!" he said with pride as he came over to Ralph.

In his hand he held a gold crucifix about three inches long. It was beautiful, the figure of Christ was studded with diamonds, but what Ralph noticed most of all were the eyes. They were a bright violet.

"There are two things that will help you," Father Ross said as he passed the crucifix to Ralph. "This will defend you. No evil will come to you as long as you wear it. The other is water blessed by a priest."

"Holy water?" quizzed Ralph.

"Yes, my son, holy water," replied Father Ross. "With holy water you can defend yourself, even attack an evil thing and drive it off."

Ralph felt a lot better. At least now he had some weapons. This he knew something about. Defence and attack. This he could relate to.

The rest of the night was spent by Ralph washing, shaving and drying his clothes. Father Ross had lent him a cassock.

Then the two men from different times talked long into the early hours.

CHAPTER THREE

Ralph slept late in to the afternoon the following day and he slept well.

Father Ross had persuaded him to sleep with the crucifix around his neck. It was the first time he had ever worn a crucifix. He wasn't a Catholic. He wasn't anything, really. His mother had sent him to Sunday school when he was young, but when she had died, his father, who was an agnostic, never pressed him to attend. But somehow the cross seemed to give a new kind of strength, an inner glow that he had never felt before.

Father Ross had put him in a small bedroom and when he awoke he was feeling much refreshed. He found that the priest had brought his clothes up to him and hung them over the edge of the bed. As he dressed he looked around at the room. There seemed to be crosses everywhere and religious pictures.

He fluffed up the mattress and made the bed. It was a habit he had picked up at Sandhurst, everything must be neat and tidy. Then he made his way down the fine oak staircase.

"Hello! Anyone there?" he called.

"This way, Master Ralph," came the reply from Father Ross.

Ralph followed the sound of the priest's voice, which seemed to come from behind the back of the staircase. Father Ross was talking to a strong-looking man who was not very tall but powerfully built. He had a mass of red hair and a beard to match. Bright blue eyes looked out from beneath a pair of bushy eye-brows.

"Ah, Master Grant! Did you sleep well?" asked the priest.

"Like a baby, Father," replied Ralph.

The priest held his hand out to the big man, and said: "This is my good friend Thommas Riddley. He looks after the church, the churchyard, the graves and he even looks after me!"

Everyone laughed.

"I am pleased to make your acquaintance," said Ralph, holding out his hand in friendship.

The big man took Ralph's hand and shook it with a grip of steel.

"The Father has told me all about you sir, and you can count on me for any help you may need."

"Thommas has been with me from the beginning," Father Ross explained, putting an arm around the big man's shoulder. "He has lent me his strength on many occasions."

"Come Master Ralph, I will show you the church before the night sets in," Thommas said, going to and opening a door that led to the outside.

"Go Master Ralph," the priest said. "He is very proud of the church, and while you are gone I will make the evening meal."

It was beautiful outside. The evening sun was sinking low in the sky and casting long shadows on everything that caught its rays. Ralph followed Thommas down the path towards the little church.

"Any historian would give his right arm to be in my position at this very moment," he thought, as he watched Thommas in his seventeenth century dress walk before him.

"Fancy not knowing of the goings-on out there for all these years. My God, what would the world give for three hundred years of peace?"

Just then Thommas stopped and held out his hand as though in warning to Ralph. He obeyed and quickly looked around but could see or hear nothing.

"What's wrong, Thommas?" he whispered to the big man.

Thommas put his forefinger to his lips demanding silence and slowly walked back to where Ralph was standing, looking all about him as he did so.

"There is something amiss here," he whispered to Ralph.

Ralph looked around again but could not see anything.

"It is too quiet," whispered Thommas. "The birds do not sing. The leaves on the trees and the tall grasses didn't move, although there is a slight breeze about. I sense the presence of evil."

Ralph looked at the things that Thommas had mentioned and he was right. A shivering feeling crept over him.

"What shall we do?" he whispered back to Thommas.

"You go back to the house and tell the Father of my fears," Thommas said quietly. "I shall go on to the church."

Ralph watched him walk slowly away. Then he hurried back to the old stone house. Father Ross was cleaning a chicken as Ralph, all out of breath, came through the door.

"Quickly, Father" he blurted out. "Thommas says that there is Evil about, near to the church."

The priest crossed himself as he dropped the chicken on to the table before running past Ralph through the open door. Ralph followed. Father Ross ran like the wind, leaving Ralph trailing behind him.

"Do you wear the crucifix, Master Ralph?" he shouted as he ran, his white hair flowing behind and his cassock billowing around him.

Before Ralph could answer there was an almighty shout from the other side of the church. The priest seemed to go even faster as he disappeared through a doorway at the bottom of the church tower.

As Ralph followed him he heard the Father shouting, his voice ringing around the little church. Thommas was standing to one side of the altar. Father Ross was in a frenzy, waving his arms about and shouting something in Latin. Ralph walked slowly towards them down a centre aisle that ran between two rows of forms. He slowed down and came to a halt when he saw what was causing the commotion.

Entrails were everywhere on the altar, hanging from statues, strewn across the altar steps. The stench was terrible, the whole lot was rotten.

"Who could have done this?" asked Ralph, as he drew near.

"It is she, that's who!" shouted Father Ross. "This is to let us know that she knows you're alive. This is only the beginning. Things will get a lot worse from now on."

"Let's get it cleared up," said Ralph, going forward.

"No, my son," replied Father Ross, standing in his way. "Thommas knows what to do. He will deal with it." And he went in to a side room. When he emerged he was carrying a chalice and he blessed its contents.

Then he proceeded to call out all the evil from the entrails by spraying holy water over the rotting innards. As the holy water reached the smelling offal it began to sizzle as though it was being cooked. Soon the little church began to smell so obnoxious that Ralph felt sick and had to run for the outside and fresh air.

Father Ross found him sitting on a tombstone. He was as white as a sheet.

"Come, my son," Father Ross said, helping him up. "Let's get away from this evil and its smell. Come up to the house, you soon will feel better."

Then he led Ralph away from the church.

It was a good two hours later when Thommas appeared, sweating and out of breath. Father Ross had saved him some food and as he tucked in to it he reported his progress to the priest.

"All is burnt and buried, Father," he said as he chewed away at a chicken leg. "All except for one small piece that I found later. I splashed it with holy water just like you did. But nothing happened. So I dug a separate hole and threw it in."

The priest didn't seem to like this but he said nothing. However Ralph could tell by his expression that something was wrong with what Thommas had done.

Ralph spent the rest of the night quietly reading some of the old books that Father Ross had collected over the years, although it was sometimes difficult to decipher some of the writers' original meaning. But he thoroughly enjoyed it.

As he sat there by the log fire, he couldn't help but notice that the priest, who was reading too, seemed preoccupied with something else. He would find him looking into the fire. His face would twitch and his eyes narrowed as though some thought of the evening's events passed through his mind.

Ralph was up early the next morning or so he thought. But when he arrived downstairs he found Father Ross in the hall pulling on a long black cloak and getting ready to go out.

"Hello!" called Ralph. "And where are you going so early in the morning?"

"I have been sorely troubled all night," replied the priest, picking up a large-brimmed black hat. "It's the thought of Thommas and these evil entrails that worries me. I must go to him at his cottage to see that he is well and no harm has come to him."

"I'll come with you," Ralph said running back up the stairs to fetch his trench coat.

It was a short walk to Thommas's cottage, a small thatched building with a neat little garden at the front.

Father Ross strode up to the front door and without knocking walked straight in. Ralph followed.

"Thommas!" he shouted. "Thommas, are you there?

A moaning noise came from a back room. The priest hurried towards it, calling:

"I'm coming, Thommas, I'm here!"

Father Ross entered a small bedroom closely followed by Ralph. The sight that met their eyes made Ralph turn away in horror.

Thommas was lying on a home-made bed beneath the window. The morning light shone through onto his writhing body. As he turned his head towards them the shining blue eyes of yesterday cried out in pain as they peered through a mass of boils and carbuncles that covered his face and head. His lips were so swollen that he could only cry out in garbled tones.

He reached out for his friend, the priest. The hand that he held towards him was also deformed with hideous swellings.

Father Ross went over, knelt by his friend and began to pray.

"What can we do?" Ralph said as he recovered from his original shock.

The priest carried on praying and did not answer him. After quite a long time he stood up and as he turned to face Ralph there were tears in his eyes.

"My good friend Thommas has left me for his maker," he said in a voice filled with emotion as he passed by Ralph and left the room.

Ralph watched the priest go and stood there not knowing what to do. He looked at the now peaceful Thommas but shuddered at the sight of his repulsive body and hurried after Father Ross.

The priest went straight to the little church and as Ralph sat watching at the back Father Ross conducted a solitary Mass for his friend.

As he sat there he wondered about the body. He would be helping if he fetched it to the graveyard and dug a grave. The priest couldn't possibly object to that.

With this in mind he slipped out of the church and made his way back to the cottage. Standing at the side of the cottage was a handcart.

"This is ideal," he thought, as he pushed it to the front door.

"What I need now is a sheet to wrap him in," he said aloud as he entered.

Rummaging around proved to be fruitless. There wasn't a thing to wrap him in, so he decided to pull him out to the cart on the mattress.

He entered the small bedroom a little apprehensive of how he could touch the festering carcass. As he slowly approached the bed he became rooted to the spot at what he saw lying there.

Instead of the strong figure of Thommas Riddley all that remained was a decomposing skeleton. Ralph turned and ran, terrified at what he had seen. He raced past a number of villagers who stood back in horror and crossed themselves at the sight of him. He ran blindly onwards up the valley to the edge of the mist. It was the mist that brought him back to his senses and he stopped, staring at the white barrier to his freedom.

"I'll have to get away from here!" he shouted at the sky "I'm going insane!" Then he fell to the ground beating his fists on the earth.

The sun was high in the sky when Father Ross found him, sitting in a peaceful meadow still looking at the mist-covered hills.

"Yes, my son," he said, as he approached. "I will have to find a way of setting you free from all this."

Ralph looked at him but didn't answer. The priest sat beside him on the grass.

"I have thought long and hard over this matter," said the priest, also looking up at the misty hills.

"I have considered the fact that if just one person, one being such as yourself, should escape from this place to the world outside and live..."

Again he paused for a while, expecting some sort of reply. But as none was forthcoming he carried on "It is my considered opinion after many years of thought and deliberation, soul-searching and prayer..."

Ralph looked up for the first time, as if to say "For God's sake, get on with it and less of the sermon!"

"...that person would break the spell for the whole valley and everything that lives here," the priest finished, looking Ralph squarely in the eyes, and that look demanded a reply.

Ralph met his stare unflinchingly and he knew by the look in the priest's eyes what it would mean.

"After seeing what I have seen today, Father," he said, "you do realise what it will mean to you and all the people here?"

"Yes, my son," the priest said standing up and looking down the Valley. "But we would be at peace. Here we are entrapped by evil," and he looked up at the sky. When he turned back to Ralph, his face shone with a deep sense of feeling.

"Up there," he shouted pointing above him. "Up there we can be free. Free to be with our friends and loved ones." And he stopped and looked at Ralph, his eyes pleading for the right reply.

Ralph stood up and faced the priest.

"I suppose one life-span should be enough for any man," he said, holding his hand out to the priest. "I'll do it."

"Praise be to God!" shouted Father Ross as he hugged Ralph to him.

"I said that you were our salvation and it has come to pass!" He carried on dancing in a circle around Ralph and waving his arms in the air.

Ralph couldn't help but laugh. If the plan worked it would benefit all concerned. Father Ross and his people would be free from their everlasting torment and he would be free to live his life as he wished.

"We must have a meeting of all the villagers," called the priest, running off down the valley.

"The time has come, the time has come!" he shouted from the distance.

Ralph watched him running first to one villager then on to another. They all seemed very excited and dashed off in different directions to tell others. Before Ralph reached the little church a large crowd had gathered outside. Father Ross came down the village street at the head of another band, all singing and laughing.

The priest pushed his way to the front and held up his arms for silence. The villagers quietened down to listen.

"My children," he called to them. "My children, the time has come for us to leave, to be united with our loved ones in Heaven."

The people looked at each other and nodded their heads in approval.

"No more shall we walk this earth forever, trapped by that evil woman. Our day is nigh," the priest shouted.

The villagers cheered and clapped as Ralph watched, although they didn't know that he was to be their saviour.

That evening Father Ross held a special Mass for the whole village. Afterwards he gathered together all the men and told them of his plan.

Each man was to go to his dwelling and make a large wooden cross, a cross as tall as a man. When this was done they were to bring it to the church and wait there.

For the next few hours the village resounded to the sounds of hammering. Soon, one by one the village men appeared at the little church carrying the results of their labour. By the time they had all congregated there were sixty wooden crosses leaning against the church wall.

Father Ross held a small service and blessed all the crosses. He then led the men out, each carrying his cross. Ralph walked with the priest at their head. Through the village street the strange procession wended its way. The women joined in, each carrying a torch.

Up towards the hills they went in complete silence, some holding hands with their partners. They had no idea what would happen to them. They only knew what Father Ross had told them and they were content to leave their fate in his hands.

Soon the procession came to a halt. The priest passed down the line talking to each and every one of them, giving instructions and blessings to all. In front of them was the mist, and at a given signal each couple carrying a cross and a torch passed into it.

Father Ross came over to where Ralph was standing. His face was grim and without a word he looked to see if Ralph wore his gold and diamond-studded crucifix. When he saw it he nodded in approval and took him by the arm into the mist.

It was as dense as he remembered it. Visibility was only a few feet either way. Father Ross led him straight up a steep climb. Halfway up a villager and his wife stood holding a cross and a torch. This went on for twenty crosses and twenty torches. The whole thing seemed too easy to him. But still it went on, until there were ten crosses and ten torches to point the way.

Ralph had counted each and every one of them.

"That was number fifty," he said quietly to the priest.

The grip on his arm became tighter as Father Ross said.

"Courage, my son not far now."

No sooner had he uttered these words when the ground began to tremble and shake. Ralph looked in horror at the priest. Parts of the hill side were opening up right in front of their eyes. The mist was moving faster and swirling about them as though it were alive.

"Run, my son!" shouted Father Ross, giving Ralph an almighty push. "Run for your life and all of ours!"

Ralph sprinted forward, leaping over a wide fracture that suddenly appeared under his feet. He kept on as straight as he could, running, jumping first this way and then that. It reminded him for a split second of France when he was on the Somme. In a short time he had seen crosses and torches scattered all over the place. The villagers that had held them had disappeared from sight.

Before he knew it he had cleared the summit and was running, falling, scrambling downwards... Suddenly there was nothing under his feet. He was falling into inky black space. His body bounced from rock to rock and he had lost consciousness by the time he hit the bottom.

The next thing he heard was a mumble of voices. He opened his eyes to a blurred vision of someone looking into his face. The voice was becoming clearer.

"Yes, he's coming round," said a man's voice.

"Thank God for that, it's about time. He had me worried," replied the soft voice of a woman.

His vision was clearing. The man looking at him wore a stethoscope around his neck.

"Now then, young fella," he said. "Can you see me?"

He passed his hand across Ralph's eyes.

"Yes," Ralph replied, weakly.

"You've had a lucky escape, my lad," continued the doctor.

"He'll be all right in about a week," he said to the woman. "It's very good of you to help him. Are you sure that I shouldn't send for an ambulance?"

"Oh, I'll enjoy looking after him," replied the woman. "He reminds me of my Tom when he was his age. He'll be no trouble at all."

"Right then," the doctor said, putting his stethoscope into his bag. "I'll see you tomorrow, Polly. If you need me, you know where I am."

The doctor left, followed by the woman. He could hear them talking as they made their way down a flight of rickety wooden stairs.

Ralph lay there wondering what had happened to him. Had he been wounded in battle? No, the doctor was a civilian. Then where was he? And who was that woman?

His brain began to clear. He remembered running and falling. Then he remembered from what and all that had happened before. He tried to sit up but a pain in his side held him back.

"Now, young man, we'll soon have you up and about," said the woman as she came into the room and pulled up a chair beside the bed.

"I want to know all about you and what in heaven's name you were doing at the bottom of Bamford's Crack in the middle of the night!"

Ralph told her that his name was Grant and he had been on a rambling holiday. He had just crossed the valley on the other side of the high hill when he fell.

The woman, who was short and dumpy and whose face had a real country-fresh look, started to laugh.

"There's no valley over the high hills, you silly lad!" she cried. "You're pulling Old Polly's leg, you are. Why that's Bamford's Lake, it's known round here as 'Squire's Pond,'" and she roared with laughter.

Ralph was confused by this statement.

"You mean there's neither a valley, nor a village, over those hills?" he asked, looking puzzled.

"Some say that there used to be a village there, many many years ago," the woman replied. "Some say that you can hear the church bell ringing on a calm peaceful night."

"Mrs…?" Ralph began, but he was cut short by the woman.

"Oh I'm not a 'Mrs,'" she laughed. "I'm Miss Polly Riddley. I live here with my brother. We've lived here all our lives, as our fathers have before us for generations. It's a very old local name, you know."

Ralph couldn't believe it when he heard the name. But he held back from saying anything about Thommas.

"This Bamford name keeps coming up," he said. "Why is that, Polly?"

"Why, there used to be Bamford's here hundreds of years ago," she replied. "They do say that Lady Bamford, the last one that is, was some sort of a witch. It was she that ended the family line, so to speak. You can still see the ruins of the great Manor House sticking up out of the water in Bamford's Lake."

Ralph looked at the ceiling and thought "Did I dream it all while I've been unconscious? But it was all so real. Father Ross, Thommas Riddley, the people, the little church, the village..?"

Then something hit him like a bolt out of the blue:

"The Cottage!" he shouted, frightening Polly out of her wits.

And he knew that he hadn't been dreaming.

CHAPTER FOUR

Ralph found out later from Polly that he had been out cold for two days. So only God knows how long he had been down at the bottom of Bamford's Crack, which was a deep narrow gorge half-way down the hillside.

The doctor had been again the following day and explained his injuries to him: three broken ribs, a fractured collarbone and twenty stitches for lacerations. He had indeed been lucky.

As he lay there in Polly's cosy bedroom he had plenty of time to think. He could remember everything about the village in detail and everything that had happened there. He was more than convinced that he had been there and experienced the whole thing. Nobody would convince him otherwise.

He remembered the crucifix and looked quickly around the room. His clothes were lying over the back of a chair.

"It must be there," he said aloud, trying to move.

He managed to swing his legs out of the bed. Trying to stand up was something else. The pains in his chest were agony he could hardly breathe. Holding onto the end of the bed with his good left arm he tried to reach out for the chair with his right leg. Just then the door opened and in came Polly.

"My God, Ralph," she cried. "What do you think you're doing?" Then she turned to the open door, shouting: "Tom, Tom! Come quickly!"

Polly came over to him and tried to help him back to the bed. But she was so small that it was useless. There was the sound of heavy footsteps coming up the stairs, and through the doorway came Polly's brother Tom.

The sight of him gave Ralph a shock. For he was the image of Thommas Riddley from the village.

"Now then, what's going on 'ere?" he said, taking hold of Ralph and helping him back to bed.

Ralph couldn't take his eyes off him. His red hair, his bushy eyebrows, his stocky frame, everything about him. He was the old Thommas all over again.

"Now what were you up to, you young rascal?" scolded Polly as though she was chastising a naughty boy.

"I wanted something from my clothes," Ralph said, trying to catch his breath. "It's something important to me."

"There's nothing in your clothes," replied Polly, going over to a chest of drawers. "All your belongings are in here," she said, pulling one of the drawers open and handing Ralph a paper bag. 'That's all you had on you when Tom brought you here."

"I'm very grateful to you, Tom," said Ralph, rummaging through the bag and triumphantly pulling out the gold and diamond-studded crucifix.

"There it is!" he cried. "I knew it, I knew that I'd been there and this proves it!"

"Yes, all right," said Polly, pulling the bedclothes around him and playing down whatever he was going on about.

"Now that you've got it I hope that you will stay put in this bed. That could have been very serious if you had fallen over, me lad."

Ralph wasn't listening to a word she was saying. All he could do was look at the crucifix and smile.

It was several days before Ralph was able to walk unaided. But when he did he found that he was on a small farm. Polly, who was in her late fifties, looked after the domestic animals and the farm, while Tom cared for the sheep up in the hills.

He couldn't wait to climb up to the top of that hill again. He wanted to see for himself what was over there. So one morning two weeks later, after the doctor had been for the last time, he set off without telling Polly where he was going.

It was a good two-hour climb to the top and as he breasted the rise his heart beat faster not knowing what lay in store for him on the other side. But all his hopes of seeing the village were dashed as he looked down on the grey waters of Bamford's Lake.

Sitting by the lake's edge he scanned the water in search of the ruins that Polly had mentioned. He spotted them over to his right and decided to have a closer look.

As he got nearer, he could see dark grey stones sticking out of the water. He was fascinated by them and tried to get nearer still, when a cool breeze sprang up, making him lift his head to look at the weather.

Black clouds were approaching from the other side of the lake. The calm waters of a few minutes' ago were now rough. The wind was getting stronger and rain was starting to come down hard, cold stinging rain that hurt his skin.

He looked again at the ruins and to his horror a mist was forming around them, a mist whipped up by the strong wind and coming straight towards him. He backed slowly away, keeping his eyes firmly fixed on the swirling mist. Then he stopped and listened. He heard the sound of a bell coming across the stormy water as it was carried on the wind. It was as though a warning was being issued to him. He waited no longer. Scrambling up to the top, he was soon safely on his way back to the farm.

That night as he lay in his snug warm bed listening to the storm buffeting against the window, he realised that all was not over yet. Danger still lurked up there in the hills and he didn't want it brought down on Polly and her brother Tom. Come morning he was going to leave.

Ralph told Polly the next morning at breakfast. She didn't like it but she understood that a young lad like Ralph wanted young company. It wasn't any good for a young fellow being stuck in the wilds.

He kissed her goodbye and set off for Keswick vowing to return in the not too distant future.

Managing to hitch a lift on a farmer's cart going to Keswick market was a bonus. It would give him enough time to get to the bank. He had arranged facilities before leaving the sanatorium.

Ralph was standing at the bank counter waiting far the teller to count his money when a man dashed in, shouting: "It's over! The war's over!"

Everybody looked at each other in disbelief, then after a few seconds the whole place erupted. Everyone began cheering and hugging each other. Women were crying. Outside in the street the whole population of Keswick was going wild.

He left the bank and entered into the celebrations. The scars on his face didn't seem to matter any more. Women kissed him, men shook him by the hand. Flags seemed to appear from nowhere, hanging from every window. The display of patriotism was outstanding, making him feel very proud.

Getting to the station was proving to be difficult. He could hardly move two or three yards without someone accosting him, one way or the other. Even when he did eventually arrive there, it was just the same.

The man in the ticket office gave him a ticket to Penrith for nothing. He wouldn't hear of him paying for it.

"The world's gone mad!" he thought as he sat in the waiting room.

It was half an hour before the little local train with its tall smoke-stack came puffing into the station. Ralph strolled onto the platform not expecting to meet any one that he knew, when someone shouted:

"Hey there, Grant, isn't it?"

Ralph turned to see William Sittwell, an ex-captain of his old regiment, waving to him from farther down the platform.

"Well, I'll be blowed!" Sittwell called as he ran up to him. "Fancy meeting you here, Ralph, old boy. Wonderful news, isn't it? The war and all that, what?"

Ralph could never stand William Sittwell. He was a pompous bore. His family had lots of money and he let everyone know it. He had never done a day's work in all of his life, but Ralph tried to look pleased to see him.

"Sittwell! How nice to see you again!" he said, shaking his hand. "And where are you off to?"

Sittwell, who was a tall thin man in his late twenties, also had a thin gaunt face to match. But a huge Roman nose protruded from it and together with his little beady eyes he looked like a stork to Ralph. His fair hair had receded so far back that it was hardly visible.

"Actually old chap," Sittwell replied, looking around as though someone might be listening, "actually I'm off for a jolly holiday..." and he gave Ralph a wink.

"Oh I see," answered Ralph "Anyone I know?"

Sittwell giggled like a schoolboy and looked around again before replying to the question.

"I don't know, old man," he said, still giggling. "It was all done through the post. You know, one of those correspondence things." And he gave Ralph a little push and another wink.

Ralph could hardly keep his face straight. He wanted to laugh out loud at the stupid man but the guard's whistle saved him.

"Must get going, Sittwell," he called as he boarded the train.

"I'll see you again!" shouted Sittwell dashing off along the platform.

It was a good few minutes before the train left the station but as it eventually drew away from the platform Ralph took one last look at the town and its happy people. What he saw made him gasp in horror. Sittwell was getting into a horse-drawn trap and the driver was the very same man that had taken him to the cottage.

He opened the window and shouted "Sittwell! Get out of there, you're in danger" and he waved his arms frantically at Sittwell, who waved back happily.

Ralph banged on the window in frustration as the train began to pick up speed. Sittwell had disappeared from sight and Ralph knew then that all had been in vain. She was still active, still bringing victims to the cottage.

"My God!" he cried, as he slumped back into his seat. "That means that the village must still be there. Father Ross and all those people, they went through all that for nothing."

Then, close to tears he held the crucifix tight.

He had journeyed to Penrith, changed trains to Lancaster and now he was well on his way to Crewe. He was so wrapped up in his thoughts that he never even noticed the wonderful scenery that passed him by.

On his arrival at Crewe Junction he just had time to make the connection to London. It was lucky for him that the porter had pushed him into a first class carriage next to the dining car, for within an hour he was feeling hungry.

Making his way there he seated himself at an empty table and was deeply engrossed in the menu when a female voice said: "Is there anything good on today?"

Ralph looked up, a little shocked. He had never expected anyone to sit at the same table, especially a woman, and a good-looking one at that.

She had deep red hair that touched her shoulders. Her eyes were smiling, kind and green. He had never seen such a beauty and back came all his fears.

His hand went straight up to his face and he did not answer her.

"I asked you if there was anything good in there!" she said, pointing at the menu.

Ralph did not reply. He just turned and looked out of the window.

"It's very rude not to reply when someone asks a question," she carried on, her green eyes beginning to flash. "I suppose you think that you are the only person in the whole wide world with a scar like that? Why, I've seen hundreds worse than that when I was in France during the war."

That statement shook Ralph rigid. He slowly turned and looked at her.

"Oh," he said. "And what were you doing in France, shooting with a gun?"

"There's no need to be sarcastic as well as rude," she said coldly. "For your information I was a nurse to a surgeon on the Front Line and I have been mentioned in dispatches. I've seen more blood than you've had hot dinners."

He started to laugh. He had never heard a woman talk like that before. She made him feel humble as well as giving him back his courage to look at her and he dropped his hand onto the table.

"That's better!" she said, with a twinkle in her eye. "Now will you answer the question please, Mr ...?"

"My name is Ralph Grant," he said, holding out his hand to her.

She took it and the sensation of holding her hand in his sent his heart racing.

She pulled it away and looked at him from under her lovely eyelids.

"I'm Helen Graham," she said, taking the menu from him. "Now what shall I have? I'm starving."

The meal was a complete success. He had never known anyone like her.

She made him feel whole again and he was talking like an excited schoolboy. Everything was wonderful. She changed compartments so that they could be together for the rest of the journey.

It was on the outskirts of London when Helen said "Oh, I forgot to ask you where you are staying in town."

"I've still to find somewhere," Ralph replied. "I'll put up in some hotel or other. Let me have your address then I can let you know where I am staying."

"I've been thinking," she said. "Mrs Coolridge, that's my landlady, she may have a room to let. She's a bit of a dragon, but she's harmless. What do you think?"

He could hardly contain his excitement. He couldn't think of anything more wonderful than living in the same house as Helen.

"That would be marvellous!" he cried. "Do you think she has?"

"We'll have to wait and see," she replied. "You come home with me. You can meet her and then we'll see, won't we?"

He was like a child in her hands. Christmas had come to him all in the space of four hours. He was walking on air for the first time in his life.

"Number 32 Wellington Street, please!" Helen called to the driver of the taxi. "Er -Chelsea!" she added as an afterthought.

Helen had her bags put alongside the driver and she looked puzzled when Ralph told her that his luggage had been lost. But she smiled when he asked her to help him choose some new clothes from the shops.

Wellington Street was a long quiet middle-class road full of smart houses. Each was painted in black and white and had a flight of white stone steps rising to a shiny front door with an equally shiny door knocker. Every house had a line of black painted railings at the front and a flight of steps going down to the servants' quarters in the basement.

The taxi pulled up at Number 32.

"Here we are!" Helen said, looking through the cab window.

Ralph opened the door and helped her out. She ran up the steps and knocked with the shiny knocker. Ralph paid the driver and stood with the bags on the pavement.

The door opened and there stood a small stout woman. Her hair was grey and tied in a bun at the back. Her face was podgy and her two dark brown eyes flashed between Ralph and Helen as the latter explained his predicament. It ended with Mrs Coolridge calling to Ralph:

"Don't stand there in the street young man! You'll have the neighbours talking."

Walking into the hall at Number 32 was like going into the hall of mirrors. Everything shone. The smell of furniture polish was over powering. Pictures hung everywhere over a floral wallpaper. A grandfather clock ticked solemnly next to a hall stand covered in hats and coats and a large Chinese vase displayed a multitude of umbrellas and walking sticks.

"Mrs Coolridge, this is my friend Ralph Grant," Helen said, introducing them to each other.

"How do you do?" said Ralph, feeling very nervous at meeting the dragon.

"Pleased, I'm sure," Mrs Coolridge answered, looking him up and down as though he was something she was going to buy in a shop.

"So you want to stay in my house do you, Mr Grant?" she carried on as she walked into the parlour. "Come in and sit yourselves down, there are things to discuss. I like to know all about my guests before I commit myself."

The interview was like a police cross-examination. She wanted to know all about his family. Where he was going to work? Had he enough funds to keep himself until he found employment? But everything swung his way when he told her that he was an ex-officer and the scars on his face were a result of the battle for the Somme.

Mrs Coolridge was a first class snob. It would boost her prestige with the neighbours to have a man like former Captain Ralph Grant staying under her roof.

The next three weeks were wonderful. London went mad. There were many parties to go to, shows, dances, dinners... It seemed never-ending.

Ralph had even been appointed as a visiting officer for disabled servicemen by the War Office. His cup was overflowing.

It was after one of these gay nights out that Ralph and Helen arrived back at Number 32. They found a policeman standing in the well-polished hall and he directed them into the parlour without saying a word.

The room was full of lodgers, or as Mrs Coolridge preferred to call them, "paying guests". She was in a collapsed state, lying on the settee.

"What's happened?" Helen asked her in alarm. "What's going on?"

"Oh, Miss Helen," she cried. "It's dreadful. I arranged for Mr Lomas in the room next to yours to change rooms with Captain Ralph as a surprise for the Captain, so that he could be next door to you."

"That was very good of you, Mrs Coolridge!" Ralph said, getting agitated. "But what's happened?"

"We managed to get it done while you were out," she sobbed. "Mr Lomas was quite happy with your attic room and I left him there setting things out. About an hour later I went up to see if everything was satisfactory. When I arrived at his door there was a horrific noise coming from the room. I banged on the door but it just went on and on. It was terrible. I was frightened out of my wits. So I sent for the police."

"But what has happened to Mr Lomas?" asked Helen.

"I don't know," replied Mrs Coolridge still sobbing. "The police are up there now but they haven't told us anything. They just told us all to come into here and wait."

"I'll try to find out what's going on," Ralph said to Helen as he opened the parlour door.

Outside in the hall the policeman came over to Ralph.

"Did you want something, sir?" he said in a superior manner.

"Who's in charge?" asked Ralph in his best army voice.

The officer seemed to come to attention as he recognised an officer.

"Inspector Sharp, sir," came the smart reply.

"I'd like to speak to him, please," Ralph said politely.

"Sergeant!" the constable called up the stairs.

The fat moustached face of the sergeant popped over the bannister rail.

"There's a gent down here would like a word with the Inspector!" called the constable.

"Better send him up then, hadn't you, Simkins," came the reply from the sergeant.

Ralph climbed the stairs to the first landing. The sergeant was standing further along barring his way.

"So you want to see the Inspector do you, sir?" the sergeant said, folding his arms and giving Ralph a good looking over.

"I want to know what's happening up there," said Ralph. "That's my room and I demand to know what's going on."

There was a noise on the upper staircase.

"Well you'll soon find out, sir," the sergeant replied. "Here's the Inspector now."

A very large man well over six feet tall and weighing a good eighteen stones, wearing a brown suit with a bowler hat to match and sporting a handlebar moustache, waddled towards them.

"This gentleman wants a word, Inspector," the sergeant said. "He says that's his room up there."

"And what's your name, sir?" the Inspector said, in a deep gruff voice.

Ralph introduced himself and explained about the exchange of rooms. He also told the Inspector that whatever had happened up there wasn't meant for Mr Lomas but for him.

The Inspector's droopy eyelids fluttered a little at this statement. It was his only sign of interest. His big sorrowful brown eyes looked at Ralph for a moment before he replied.

"I think you had better come with me, sir," he said with a sigh, as he looked at the long flight of stairs.

Inspector Sharp was left puffing and panting as they reached the attic landing. Another policeman was standing outside the attic door.

"Now then, Mr Grant," puffed the Inspector, "before we go in there I must warn you that it isn't very pleasant."

Ralph nodded and waited for the constable to open the door. He was expecting something horrible but as the door swung inwards the sight that met his eyes had him rooted to the spot.

There were bloodstains everywhere even on the ceiling. The furniture was smashed to pieces; the once neat bedclothes were bloodstained and ripped into shreds. A human leg could be seen sticking out from under the debris.

Ralph felt sick and looked at the Inspector.

"If you think this was meant for you, Mr Grant," said Inspector Sharp, "then you should thank your lucky stars that you were not here when whatever it was came to call."

"I've never seen anything so macabre!" Ralph said taking two more steps forward.

"I'm afraid you haven't seen it all yet," the Inspector said, pointing to a corner. "Go on, Mr Grant, have a look, you might as well."

Ralph went over to where the Inspector was pointing. He pulled away a piece of smashed furniture revealing a battered torso.

"My God!" he cried, as he dropped the splintered wood and turned away in horror. "What could have done such a thing?"

"God knows, Mr Grant," replied Inspector Sharp. "Whatever it was, I don't want to meet it. You see, it was bloody clever as well."

"How do you mean, Inspector?" asked Ralph, making his way to the door.

"Well, you see, Mr Grant, it's like this," the Inspector began. "Whatever was in this room not only ripped this man apart limb from limb but did it all behind a locked door and a nailed-up window frame. When it had finished its slaughter it disappeared without trace into thin air!"

"But how?" quizzed Ralph.

"Not only did it disappear," the Inspector carried on ignoring Ralph's question, "it took the man's head with it."

Ralph's mouth dropped open when he heard this and he opened the door to the landing. He had seen enough.

The Inspector followed him, still talking.

"We have been over that room with a fine-tooth comb, Mr Grant," he said. "And there's no way anything could have got out. There isn't a spot of blood out here on the landing. The landlady Mrs Coolridge was standing in the hall all the time it was going on. Nothing came down the stairs. It has us completely baffled."

Ralph made a move to go down the stairs but the Inspector stopped him.

"Just a moment, Mr Grant," he said, taking hold of his arm. "Before you go I want you to promise me that you won't say a word to a soul about what you have seen here tonight. If this gets out the whole of London will be in panic. What's in that room is far worse than what Jack the Ripper did. Do you understand?."

Ralph gave his word. He couldn't do anything else. If he had told the Inspector what he thought had done it, an evil monster sent from hell, they would have sent for a straitjacket.

CHAPTER FIVE

For the next few days the house was never free from the comings and goings of the police. Ralph tried to keep away as much as he could. He took Helen out as usual but his heart wasn't in it. The terrible slaughter at Number 32 was always at the back of his mind.

To consolidate his defences against such an attack he called to see the local priest and acquired a large bottle of holy water. With this deposited around his room in small dishes he felt much safer. He also filled a small bottle which he kept on his person at all times.

Ralph was thoroughly enjoying his job and during his travels in and around London visiting old soldiers he had started to frequent a small tea shop which was run by two old ladies. The shop was in Baylis Road, Lambeth and whenever he was in the district he could be found there between ten and eleven o'clock in the morning drinking a cup of tea and reading the morning paper.

It was on a cold damp December morning when the London fog was at its worst. Visibility was down to a few yards and Ralph had lost patience with it. He had tried several times to find an old soldier's address but he always ended up getting lost. Realising that he was in the locality he headed for the tea shop.

Sitting at his favourite table drinking a warming cup of tea and reading his morning paper was Ralph's idea of heaven. The little tea shop was quite full. The notorious fog had driven in more customers than usual.

He had been there about half an hour. The chattering of the extra customers didn't bother him but something did. He had the feeling that he was being watched. The hairs on his neck began to tingle. The feeling was so strong that as he tried to pick up his cup his hand shook, spilling tea over the neat table-cloth. He felt so embarrassed when the waitress changed it, it seemed that everyone in the tea shop was looking at him. Rather than look around at the faces of the patrons he stared out of the window at the fog. But the feeling persisted, getting stronger and stronger until he started to shake. Sweat was pouring from him.

Whatever it was that made him frightened, it wasn't human and he knew it. Something evil was in the tea shop and he knew that he had to face it.

Fingering the crucifix he decided to make a dash for the door.

“The thing won’t dare to attack me in a public place,” he thought.

Making up his mind he suddenly turned and in doing so he knocked over the tea pot which in turn knocked over the cup and saucer. The latter fell to the floor and shattered into many pieces, making all the customers stop what they were doing and stare at him.

He didn’t care any more, getting out of there was his prime objective. Running wildly between the tables and chairs, banging into people in his blind panic, he managed to reach the door only to stop dead in fright. For there sitting at the nearest table to the door was Mary Bamford, the Lady of the Manor herself, her long golden hair cascading over her white dress.

Ralph was petrified he just stood and stared, his eyes wide with fright.

“I have come for you, Ralph,” she said in a voice that made him tremble from head to foot. “Did you think that you could run away from me?” and she started to laugh a hideous cackling laugh.

Ralph pointed at her but couldn’t speak. Then a cry came from him as he dashed out into the fog.

The people in the little tea shop were all standing up watching him, and as he disappeared into the fog they all started to talk loudly.

“Did you see that?” said one old man. “He was frightened to death. The poor fella was pointing at that table as though there was somebody there. But it’s empty.”

“It’s the war,” said another. “That’s what it does to some of them.”

Ralph was running for his life, not knowing where or in which direction. The thick London fog seemed even thicker. He ran until he could run no more.

He stopped in a near-collapsed state, gasping for breath.

“God, what am I going to do?” he cried as he gulped in great quantities of smutty London fog.

“She could be anywhere!” he cried frantically, looking around him into the grey wall of mist. “This is her domain, she thrives in these conditions.”

He was at his wits end, not knowing which way to turn, when he felt a hard object in his pocket.

“The holy water!” he gasped as his fingers closed around the small bottle. “I’d forgotten about it” he said pulling it out gently and looking at it. “I hope Father Ross was right about this stuff. Now if it was a hand grenade I could understand that. But it's only water blessed by a priest. How can this defeat the likes of her and the demons she can conjure up?"

He had been in the same spot for about half an hour and nothing had happened to him. He was beginning to get his courage back. There were a few people walking about and he decided to ask for directions.

As he stood there waiting a figure loomed up out of the fog. The frame, stature and dress he knew only too well, a long black cloak, white hair and, as the figure came nearer, the face.

"Father Ross! Father Ross!" he called out, holding out his arm towards the priest. But as the priest passed him Ralph's out-stretched arm went straight through the figure. He couldn't believe it and turned quickly to see where Father Ross had gone.

The spectre of the priest was standing a few yards away in the fog beckoning him to follow.

Ralph was frightened, his instincts told him to run. But something deep down said "trust it and follow." So gathering up all his courage and holding tight to the holy water he walked towards the spectre. The spectre in turn walked on ahead.

They seemed to have walked quite a way, though in the fog he couldn't tell, when the spectre turned into an alley way. When Ralph turned the same corner it had gone. He looked around expecting something to happen. But nothing did.

Walking a few more yards into the alley he could see a light shining through the fog. He became curious and went on. He found that the light was hanging over an old shop. It was straight from Dickens: Georgian bowed window and all. The windows were dirty and whatever was on display was hard to see. Ralph rubbed at one of the small panes of glass and putting his face right up to it he could just make something out.

"Books," he muttered in a puzzled way. But then he saw what kind of books they were.

"Religious books!" he cried, standing back and looking up at the dirty sign over the shop. "The Theologian," he read out loud.

"Father Ross must have led me here," he said, looking the place over. "There's no other explanation."

Ralph tried the handle on the shop door. It moved. He pushed gently and the door began to open, making a creaking, squeaking noise. A solitary candle glowed on a table in the back of the shop giving the whole place an eerie atmosphere as it threw shadows across the many statues that stood around. Cobwebs hung everywhere. It looked as though the place hadn't been open for a hundred years or more.

There was a horrible musty smell in the air. Dust covered everything. Ralph slowly made his way towards the candle, knocking a passage through the cobwebs as he went. No-one had walked across that floor for years. Little clouds of dust blew up around his feet with each step that he took.

"Phew, what a place!" he grumbled, knocking down the last cobwebs before he reached the candle.

"There must be someone here for that to be lit," he thought looking at the light.

"Hello, is anyone there?" he called. There was no response except for the dust falling from the cobwebs higher up as his voice resounded around the little shop.

As he looked around, still expecting someone to come in, he noticed that there were shelves full of books further back in the shadows and a door that led to the back of the shop.

"Hello!" he called again and again the dust gently floated down, followed by the same deathly silence.

"There must be someone here," he thought, making his way around the table to the door. But the door was covered with cobwebs and he knew that no-one had come through it for years.

Turning back again to the light he noticed a book lying next to the candle.

"That's strange," he said. "That wasn't there before, I'm sure of it."

He went over and looked down at the book.

"I knew it!" he gasped. "This has just been put here. It's clean with not a speck of dust on it."

He looked towards the shop door but the his own telltale foot prints on the floor told him that no-one had followed him in.

Ralph picked the book up. He was trembling with excitement as he took it nearer the light. It was a volume covered in brown leather and quite heavy. The title was embossed in gold letters and his heart jumped for joy as he read: *The Destruction of Witches and Daemons, Father James Ross, 1654.*

He flicked through the fading pages but suddenly the candle flickered and went out. It frightened him for a moment but he soon regained his composure. As he went out of the little shop, hugging the book close to his chest, he turned and said a quiet "thank you" to the darkness.

Outside in the alleyway the fog was lifting and as he approached the corner to the street he noticed a sign on the wall.

"St Peter's Place," he said aloud. "I'll never forget that as long as I live."

It was mid-afternoon when he arrived back at Wollington Street.

Helen wasn't at home and he was glad of that. He wanted to read the book and he didn't want any distractions in that direction. Hurrying to his room he locked the door and excitedly opened Father Ross's book.

To his horror it was mostly written in an old style of English, but as he read on he found that he could understand most of it.

The Father gave accounts of certain witches of his time, notably a noblewoman called Frances Howard who later became the Countess of Sumerset. She had her first husband murdered in The Tower of London by a woman known as Anne Turner. The same Anne Turner was hanged but the Countess being high-born was set free.

The Pendle witches were mentioned and the trials of 1612. Elisabeth Southerns known as Old Demdike, Elisabeth Device, Anne Whittle, Alias Chattax, they were all there. It made fascinating reading. There was a passage on how to detect a witch. They could be trough-eyed (he took this to mean a squint); they had Devil marks on their bodies which could be found in their secret places; a witch finder must be employed to seek them out. When pricked these marks did not bleed. Ralph found all this very absorbing but very hard to believe. But then he came upon the name Mary Bamford and the Father's writing became different, more serious. He could feel the passion in his words. The Father gave details of her beauty. He told the whole story of how she became the temptress and seductress of the valley. He listed the names of all the unfortunate men and young boys who had died at her hands.

But Ralph knew all this. None of this was new. It wouldn't help him in his present predicament. But all this changed when he read of how Father Ross used holy water to good effect. He seemed to have done everything with it, from sprinkling it around the house to washing his clothes in it, swearing that it gave him an armour-like protection. This gave Ralph something to build on. There could be numerous ways of exploiting this. He was feeling much better now that he had something. The more he thought about it the better he felt. Just to have the book there was enough but the ideas it was giving to him made him realise that he had more than a fighting chance of winning, more than a chance of coming out of this alive.

As he reached the end of the priest's wonderful book. His courage and determination had returned.

At the end of the book he came across a few lines of verse which he read aloud.

"If thou gazest on the Devil's daughter

Gird thyself with cross and water

The Lord will stand as thy protector

And guard thee from

The Devil's spectre."

This seemed to sum up all that the book had to say. He closed it and gently stroked it, remembering how fearless Father Ross had been when they last met on that fateful night when he and all the villagers sacrificed themselves for him.

It was a week before Christmas. Ralph and Helen had been out shopping for presents. About seven in the evening Mrs Coolridge answered a knock at the front door. She came into the parlour looking very puzzled and carrying a hat-box.

"Someone has left this on the front step," she said. "It's addressed to you, Miss Helen," and she put the box on the table.

"For me?" Helen said, getting up from her chair. "How strange! Fancy someone doing a thing like that."

Ralph, who liked a doze after his evening meal, suddenly realised that something could be wrong.

"Don't touch it!" he called out to Helen and dashed across the room, snatching the hat-box from the table.

"Whatever is the matter?" she said in alarm. "Don't be silly, Ralph, give it to me. After all it is addressed to me, isn't it?"

"You can't be too careful," he replied. "Not after what happened to Mr Lomas upstairs."

"What do you mean?" asked Mrs Coolridge.

"Yes, what do you mean?" butted in Helen. "What exactly did happen upstairs? You never did tell us."

Ralph could have bitten his tongue out. He didn't know what to say. How could he tell them: he couldn't break his word to Inspector Sharp and yet he would look a fool if there was a hat in the box. But he couldn't take the risk and he stuck to his guns.

"I'll tell you one day," he said. "But I must let the Inspector look at this first. You might think I'm being silly but I appeal to you not to judge me too harshly." He carried the hat-box out of the room, leaving the two women dumbfounded.

Half an hour later Ralph was walking into Scotland Yard and asking for Inspector Sharp. He was shown into an ante-room to wait. It was a good hour later before he was summoned before the Inspector.

"Ah, Mr Grant!" greeted the Inspector as Ralph entered his office. "Please sit down. I'm sorry for keeping you so long. What can I do for you?."

"It's this," Ralph said, putting the hat-box on the Inspector's desk. "It was left on the door step at Number 32 Wellington Street at approximately seven o'clock tonight."

"What's in it?" asked the inspector.

"I don't know," replied Ralph. "I haven't opened it. It's addressed to Miss Helen. But I think it's more sinister than a hat. That's why I brought it to you."

"We'll soon find out, won't we, Mr Grant!" the Inspector said, picking up the box and untying the ribbon around it.

Ralph leaned across the desk to get a better view. The Inspector lifted the lid and took out a piece of tissue paper before he could see what the box contained. He looked at what was in the box for a few seconds and then pushed it across the desk to Ralph without batting an eye-lid.

It only took a glance into the box to tell Ralph that he had been right in not letting Helen open it. For there staring up at him was the decomposing head of Mr Lomas.

He looked across at the Inspector and when their eyes met he knew what the questions would be.

"Well, Mr Grant, this poses me a real problem, doesn't it?" said the Inspector stroking his moustache.

"In the first place how did the head get out of the room? And in the second why was it returned and by whom? The third thing that worries me: why was it addressed to your Miss Helen?"

Ralph sat there, fighting with his conscience. After a while he banged his fist on the desk and jumped up.

"It's no good!" he stormed. "I've got to tell someone or I'll go mad!"

The Inspector, cool as ever, just looked at him and did not answer.

"You'll never believe it. It's a crazy story," he cried walking about in front of the desk. "You'll think I'm raving, only fit for the asylum!"

"Let me be the judge of that, Mr Grant," replied the Inspector quietly. "Now sit down and take it easy, man. There's no need to get excited."

Ralph did as he was told and soon regained his composure. The Inspector sent for a pot of tea. The head was removed and Ralph began his story.

Two hours and several cups of tea later, Ralph had finished his sordid tale. The Inspector had listened with ever-increasing interest, making notes at every opportunity.

When all was done the Inspector just sat there thinking. Ralph was waiting for his opinion, in trepidation.

"Mr Grant," he said at last. "I am not a true believer in the church or the Devil for that matter, but after what I saw at 32 Wellington Street and the disappearance of the head, I must confess that there is no other natural conclusion I can come to. Your story gives credence to what happened there and I have no other option than to believe you."

Ralph could have jumped for joy. At last he had someone that he could talk to and confide in. Perhaps help was at hand at last.

"There is just one thing that I want you to do, Mr Grant," said the Inspector. "This must be kept just between you and me. I have to think what it would do to my reputation at the Yard if it got out."

"You don't have to worry about that!" laughed Ralph, relieved that everything was out in the open at last.

"There are one or two things that need clearing up," the Inspector said, putting his overcoat on and getting ready to leave.

"I'll want to see that old book and I'll have to check on the old shop in St Peter's Place."

Ralph nodded in agreement.

"The other things I'm afraid are up to you, Mr Grant," the Inspector carried on. "Your Miss Helen, I think she should be told."

Ralph looked at him in alarm.

"Now before you say anything, hear me out," the Inspector said, leading Ralph to the door.

"It's getting late," he said as they walked down the passage that led to the outside. "I have a car at my disposal. I'll take you to Wellington Street and we can talk on the way."

The Inspector dispensed with the services of the driver because he didn't want anyone to hear their conversation and as he drove along he explained his theory to Ralph.

"You see," he said, "I look at it this way, Mr Grant. Someone is getting at you through Miss Helen and I think she has the right to the same defences that you have. That means that you will have to tell her all about it and from what I've seen of that young woman it wouldn't be a bad thing. She has plenty of guts and could be of great help to you."

Ralph sat there listening. What the Inspector was saying made sense. But he still didn't relish the thought of telling Helen.

"The other thing that has me worried," the Inspector carried on, "is that fellow Sittwell. I can't help wondering what's happened to him. I'll have to check him out at the Yard. If he hasn't returned from the Lake District, I wonder if would it be possible for you to go and find out."

Ralph's face showed the Inspector what he thought of that idea.

"You mean go back to the cottage?" he replied in alarm.

"You're better equipped than you were before," the Inspector said, turning the car into Wellington Street. "I'm sure an ex-Captain like you could come up with a good plan of campaign. It might be the very place to defeat this woman. Anyhow, think it over and let me know your decision. But don't under any circumstances do anything without first telling me. Is that understood, young man?" he said, leaning across Ralph to open the car door.

Ralph stood on the pavement and watched the Inspector drive away, wishing that he had never met Jack Ryan. If it hadn't have been for him and his bloody cottage, he wouldn't be in this mess.

CHAPTER SIX

Telling Helen the full story proved easy. Ralph was amazed to find out that she was fascinated by the supernatural. She was eager to help, too eager for Ralph's liking, and he had to read the riot act to her, making sure that she realised the danger she was getting into.

Two days after the meeting with Inspector Sharp, Ralph received a note from him, delivered by a detective. He opened it, a little apprehensive of its contents and began to read.

Bad news, Mr Grant.

Number One: there's no such shop as 'The Theologian', or for that matter no such street as St Peter's Place. It was demolished in 1865 to make way for warehouses.

Number Two: There has been no sign of Mr Sittwell for five weeks. Relatives are very anxious as to his welfare. He was reported missing two weeks ago. I implore you to find him.

Sharp.

PS: Let me know when you intend to go.

Ralph showed the note to Helen and after she had read it she came and put her arms around him.

"What are you going to do?" she said softly, knowing only too well that it was a difficult decision to make.

"I'll have to go," he replied. "For all our sakes, not just for Sittwell. As the Inspector says, it could mean the end of it once and for all." And he kissed her, giving them both reassurance.

Ralph sent a telegram to Polly, asking if it would be convenient for him and his lady friend to pay a visit over Christmas.

Helen thought it was a bit cheeky, but in no time at all back came the reply.

"WOULD BE DELIGHTED STOP LOOKING FORWARD TO SEEING HER STOP POLLY."

Tickets were bought and bags were packed. The Inspector was informed and in two days they were on their way. To what, they didn't know. But what they did know was that they were together and that was all that mattered.

Polly and Tom were at the station to meet them. She had ordered a taxi to take them all to the farm. It was going to be the best Christmas she and Tom had ever had. She would make sure of that, no matter what it cost her.

Helen thought Polly was wonderful.

Although it was Christmas the farm work still had to be done, so Helen helped Polly with the chickens and the general chores around the place, while Ralph went out into the hills with Tom to look after the sheep.

Christmas Day was different. The sheep were penned up and fed early as were the rest of the animals. The rest of the day belonged to Polly, Tom and their guests. It was a good old-fashioned Christmas, the likes of which Helen and Ralph had never seen before. A blazing log fire in the grate, hot punch, plum pudding, roast goose and pork, a plate of mince pies, two bottles of home made dandelion wine and to finish brandy and a fine cigar for Ralph and Tom.

Boxing Day was similar, everyone was having such a good time that the main reason for their visit was forgotten for the time being. But not so the next day.

Ralph was up early. He was determined to go to Keswick. He wanted to hire a car so that they could move about the countryside quickly.

Helen didn't relish the idea of walking fifteen miles in mid-winter but rather than say anything she went along with the plan. A stroke of luck came their way just as they were setting off. Polly's next door neighbour, Bill Cottam, came to call. He was on his way to Keswick in his truck and offered to give them a lift. Helen was overjoyed.

On their way to Keswick, Bill Cottam, who was a talkative fellow, told them of a strange man who had been seen running around the hills. The sightings had been reported to the local police but their efforts to apprehend him had all failed. Ralph and Helen looked at each other but did not comment on the matter.

Bill, who was a typical farmer, red face, rough dress, cap pulled well down and stinking of sheep, said that he would be in town for two hours and if they couldn't get fixed up with a car he'd only be to happy to have their company back to the farm.

The only car available in Keswick was a 1910 Benz. The garage proprietor was reluctant to hire it because of the brakes but Ralph was impatient and assured him that he would drive carefully.

With the formalities over they were soon driving up into the hills.

"Do you know where the cottage is?" asked Helen.

"I've got a good idea of its location," replied Ralph, "although I'm not positive. It was dark but I remember a lot of trees and there can't be too many around these parts."

They had travelled about seven miles when the road started to narrow.

It was now little more than a track, just wide enough to take the car. Suddenly Ralph stopped.

"Look up ahead," he said. "Trees, what did I tell you? I knew I was right."

"So far, so good," Helen replied, a little apprehensive. For although she had been keen at the start now that she thought things were about to happen she wasn't so sure.

Ralph started off towards the trees. They were on both sides of the track like an avenue, tall firs, thirty to forty feet high. Fifty yards into the avenue a strong wind began to blow. The trees were swaying, bending and twisting. Suddenly there was a brilliant flash of lightning. It struck into a tree twenty yards in front of them, bringing down branches that were burning.

"My God!" cried Helen, "Let's get out of here."

Ralph stopped and threw the car into reverse. There were three more flashes in quick succession, each one getting nearer to them.

"For God's sake, Ralph!" screamed Helen. "Do something!"

Ralph was finding it difficult backing the car down the track. It was so narrow that he was frightened of crashing into the trees behind them.

"Hurry!" screamed Helen, nearly out of her mind as a large burning tree came crashing down only feet from the car.

The whole avenue in front of them was ablaze but still the lightning flashed, sending more and more trees crashing down. A great ball of fire came rushing towards them just as Ralph edged past the last of the trees which were already on fire.

At a safe distance from the fire Ralph stopped the car. Helen flung her arms around him.

"Thank God!" she cried. "I thought we were going to die."

"It's all right, love," said Ralph, comforting her. "We're out of it now."

As they sat there holding each other, Ralph looked up the track at the burning trees and he suddenly realised something.

"Hold on," he said as he moved away from Helen. "That's strange."

And he got out of the car and walked a few yards down the track towards the fire. He turned back towards the car shouting.

"Look at that. There's not a cloud in the sky. I can see for miles from here."

Helen came to join him and they stood there in amazement.

"There's only one explanation for this," Ralph said, walking back to the car. "It's a warning from her. She doesn't want us anywhere near that cottage."

"You're not serious?" Helen replied, climbing up alongside him.

"Believe me, love, I'm very serious," he said, starting the car up and continuing to back down the narrow track.

"There must be some other reason, surely?" Helen asked, still unconvinced that something like that could happen because of a supernatural being.

"I have seen what this woman can do," he shouted over the noise of the engine. "I have felt her power, believe me, I know."

Just then they passed a track that ran off to the right. Ralph stopped the car again.

"I wonder where that leads to?" he said.

Helen did not reply, she was still thinking about what he had said. Without more ado he swung the car onto the unknown track.

"It must lead somewhere," he called to Helen, "and there's only one way to find out."

The new track was even worse than the old one. It had large pot-holes and ran downwards between two steep cliffs. The further they went along it the steeper became the incline.

"Do be careful, Ralph, please," Helen called out to him.

Suddenly the dirt track ran into a deep trench. The track was now rock, with great ruts in it. The trench had been cut out of high sandstone that towered on either side of them. The trench twisted first one way then another. Ralph wrestled with the wheel as the car was flung from side to side, smashing into the stone walls.

"Climb into the back," shouted Ralph "I'm losing control!"

Helen did as she was told with much difficulty. The canvas top on the car was ripped off. Helen screamed and threw herself onto the floor.

The floor of the trench became even steeper. The noise of the car smashing against the walls was horrifying and sparks were flying everywhere.

Ralph tried the brakes for the umpteenth time but there was nothing there. Suddenly the trench widened. The car was hurtling at breakneck speed onto the floor of a chasm and right in front of them was the entrance to a large cave.

"Get down!" shouted Ralph at the top of his voice.

Seconds later there was a terrific smash, then total silence as the engine spluttered to a stop.

Ralph sat up and looked around. Everywhere was in total darkness.

"Helen, are you all right, darling?" he called.

"I think so," came a squeaky reply from the back of the wrecked car.

"We had better get out of here quickly," called Ralph. "There's a strong smell of petrol but don't rush, we don't want to cause a spark or we've had it."

Helen was out first, spark or no spark, and she was heading for the only glimmer of light that was coming from the cave entrance.

"Hey, wait for me!" called Ralph, trailing behind her.

Helen stopped just outside the cave. She looked a mess her hair was hanging down around her face. The lovely curls that she had started with had all gone.

"You crazy fool!" she shouted at him as he came up to her.

"You would take that car, wouldn't you? Oh yes, you would be careful. You were a competent driver, that's what you told the garage proprietor, didn't you? Now look at the mess were in. Smashed car, miles away from anywhere, God knows what we're going to do!" Then she burst into tears.

Ralph was just about to tell her how sorry he was when there was a tremendous explosion from inside the cave. Black smoke and fumes came pouring out of the cave entrance. The blast knocked Helen off her feet, sending her sprawling onto the dusty ground. Hundreds of bats came flying out behind the smoke, squeaking and flying about in all directions. This made it even worse.

"My God!" she screamed at Ralph. "That's it, that is the last straw, Ralph Grant. I'll never speak to you again as long as I live!"

Ralph couldn't help but laugh at her: standing there covered in dust, her hair all over the place and screaming at the top of her voice.

After the smoke had subsided Ralph went to the cave entrance and looked in. The car was burning furiously and he turned to Helen, shouting. "Come and look at this, come on, it's fantastic!"

Helen didn't want to know but when he disappeared into the cave she quickly followed shouting "Don't you dare leave me on my own..."

She came running into the cave after Ralph but she stopped dead when she saw him standing in the middle of a cathedral-like cavern.

Stalagmites rose from the floor like giant pillars. The cavern was huge, stretching back hundreds of yards.

"Isn't this marvellous!" called Ralph. "Have you ever seen anything like it?"

Helen had to agree. She soon forgot about her recent rantings and helped Ralph to find something to make a torch with. Soon they were exploring the back of the cavern each of them carrying a dried branch that they had found outside and lit from the burning car.

"Be careful," said Helen as Ralph, full of enthusiasm, pressed on ahead of her.

The floor of the cavern began to rise steeply but someone in years gone by had cut steps out of the rock making it easy for them to reach a small shelf higher up.

"Look at that over there," called Ralph from a lofty position on a rock.

"It's like a gigantic church organ," he shouted, his voice echoing around the cavern as he pointed to a cluster of huge stalactites hanging from the roof.

As there was no way to climb further up he came down and stood beside her on the shelf.

"People must have used this place at one time," he said walking around, trying to find a way off their precarious position.

"Keep away from the edge, Ralph," called Helen. "There's a steep drop on that side."

Ralph followed the only possible way off the shelf. It led to a huge boulder. A narrow path led around the side and he followed it leaving Helen alone.

"Ralph," she screamed out. "Ralph, don't leave me, please!"

A few minutes later he was back.

"Come on," he called eagerly. "Come and see what I've found."

She followed him around the boulder where the shelf widened out again. In front of them was a tunnel entrance with just enough room for a man to pass through.

"Look," he said, and gathering up some of the twigs from the floor he lit a torch in front of the opening.

The flame began to flare up and blaze.

"There's a draught coming through here," he said excitedly. "That means there must be a way out."

"I do hope you're right," she said, as she followed him into the tunnel.

The tunnel twisted and turned. Then it suddenly became wider. Ralph stopped and looked at something.

"Well, I never," he said, in surprise.

"What is it?" asked Helen from behind.

"There's a big candle standing in a niche," he replied, lighting it. "It's not been used for years, it must be very old."

"That proves it," Helen said coming up to have a look at it. "People must have used this place. I wonder what for?"

Ralph did not answer but pressed on up the passage, finding candle after candle. Soon the whole tunnel was lit up behind them.

Helen changed her torch for one of them now that there was no need for it.

He was a long way ahead of her now, lighting up the passage as he went. Suddenly there was a cry from him.

"Good God, Helen come and see this!" he shouted to her.

She quickened her pace and found him standing in a kind of an altar room. There were torches placed around the side which Ralph was busily lighting. At the far end of the room was a stone altar. Standing behind the altar was a large statue. It had a man's body and the head of some kind of animal. Smaller ones were placed around the walls in between the torches.

"This was used for Devil worship!" she gasped, looking around in wonderment.

"This must have been her inner sanctum," Ralph said. "It's much too near the valley to be anyone else's," and he walked behind the main statue.

"Here's another passage," he called out.

Helen hurried to his call. Ralph, who still had his torch, had already gone along the passage. When Helen caught up to him he had reached the end.

"There are branches and brambles covering the opening," he said, trying to pull them away. "It's not been used for donkey's years. I can see some daylight. Here, help me with this!" he said, tugging at a branch.

It didn't take them long to make a hole big enough to get through. Once outside Ralph had a quick reconnoitre. They had come out halfway up a hill. There were trees everywhere and the undergrowth was quite dense.

"I think it would be best if we went downhill," said Ralph taking Helen's hand. "It's going to be rough, so hang on, the ground falls away quite suddenly in places."

They made heavy weather of it. Helen's dress was being torn to ribbons and she stopped.

"I want to rest!" she panted. "I can't go on any longer…" and she sat down among some ferns to catch her breath.

Ralph sat down beside her. After a few minutes she looked at him and said: "Do you really think that place was her inner sanctum, as you call it?"

"There's no other explanation," he replied. "Who else but her would make a temple to the Devil in these parts?"

"It scared me stiff in there," she said, getting hold of his hand.

Then she looked up, saying: "What's that over there?"

Ralph looked in the direction that she was pointing.

"It's a house," she said, standing up. "Yes, it's a house, come on, we're saved," and she set off down the slope with Ralph in hot pursuit.

As they came nearer the dwelling Ralph suddenly realised what the place was and he dashed past Helen, grabbing her by the arm.

"Stop!" he said frantically, pulling her to the ground.

Helen looked at him in alarm and she was ready to give him a piece of her mind. But Ralph put his forefinger to his lips in a sign for silence.

"It's the cottage," he whispered.

Helen's eyes opened wide in fright and she put her hand over her mouth.

"What are we going to do?" she whispered back.

"You stay here," he said in a commanding voice, "and I mean here!" he added, pointing to the ground. "Do you understand?."

Helen nodded in reply, she was too frightened to do anything else. Ralph moved off slowly between the trees, stopping now and then to look around and occasionally turning around to reassure Helen. He was now at the edge of the wood. The cottage was twenty feet away. All seemed quiet. It looked the same as he had left it. There was the hole in the roof. One or two windows were broken, everything looked peaceful so he made a dash to the cottage wall. He moved sideways to one of the windows and had a quick look in. The place was in a mess, the large table was turned over. Cobwebs hung everywhere. It looked even worse than he remembered.

He turned and waved to Helen to come down. When she arrived at his side he whispered "We'll go around to the front, I don't think Sittwell is in there. But be quiet just in case he is."

The front door was open. Ralph went in followed by Helen, although she was a shade apprehensive about the whole thing.

The main room was just as he had seen it through the window.

"Stay here," he said to her, "while I go into the bedroom."

Helen didn't need any persuading and she moved back towards the door. Ralph pushed the bedroom door open and went inside. The room looked like a rag shop and smelled terrible. Dirty clothes were everywhere. A large trunk stood next to the filthy bed and he could see human excrement all over the place. It was nauseating and he felt sick.

He was just going to leave when the dirty pile of clothes in the corner moved and a hand came out from under them. Then there was a moan. Ralph went across and against his better judgement he tugged at the filthy rags.

There was a horrific scream and a thing that used to be a human being jumped up in front of him, frightening him out of his wits.

It was Sittwell, a poor deranged Sittwell, thinner than he had ever seen him. His cheek bones were sticking out from his face, his eyes were staring wild. A scruffy beard encircled the crazed countenance. The clothes he was wearing were no more than rags.

"It's all right, Sittwell," Ralph said softly. "It's me, Ralph Grant I'm not going to hurt you."

The sound of a human voice seemed to make him worse. He backed away into the corner and began to snarl at Ralph like a dog.

Ralph walked slowly backwards to the door, keeping his eyes firmly fixed on the wretched Sittwell. He had just set foot into the main room when the raving

Sittwell came hurtling into the room and flung himself onto Ralph's back, biting, scratching and howling like an animal.

Helen screamed and ran outside. Ralph and the deranged Sittwell rolled round and round over the floor smashing into everything in sight. Managing to stand at last, with the lightweight Sittwell still clinging to him, Ralph swung round smashing Sittwell into the stone wall of the cottage and knocking the wind out of him. He fell to the floor groaning. Ralph took his chance and dashed outside.

Helen was hiding behind a tree and called to him.

"Over here, Ralph!" she cried. "Over here!"

Ralph ran across to her and pulled her behind the tree.

"He's crazy, stark staring mad," he gasped. "The bloody swine bit me on the neck."

"Where is he now?" whispered Helen.

"He won't come here, will he?" she asked, her eyes pleading with Ralph.

"I doubt it!" replied Ralph, rubbing his neck. "I knocked the wind out of his sails."

They were just going to move away when Sittwell came running out of the cottage, screaming and shouting. He ran first one way then another, seemingly not knowing which way to go. Then he went running off, screaming, shouting and waving his arms, down into the valley below.

Ralph sank to his knees exhausted. Helen tore a piece off her petticoat and tried to clean up the wound on his neck.

"Now we know what happened to him," said Ralph as he grimaced under her touch. "That could have been me running out there, a raving lunatic. Thank God I got out in time."

CHAPTER SEVEN

Ralph and Helen arrived back at Wellington Street the day before New Year's Eve. Polly and Tom were sorry to see them go, but they had had such a good time that Ralph and Helen were invited up for Easter. The man at the garage wasn't too bothered about the car, he was well insured, and said he would buy a new one out of the proceeds.

The Inspector was told the full story about William Sittwell and he instigated a full search for him but Ralph didn't hold out much hope of him being found.

There was to be a grand dinner and ball on New Year's Eve. It was being given by the War Office staff, generals included, and it was to be held at an old country house somewhere near Aylesbury. The old house had been taken over by the General Staff during the war and this was to be a last fling before handing it back to the real owner.

Helen and Ralph had been invited and they were to be picked up by a Commander Reg Mills RNVR and his wife at six o'clock sharp. Helen was a bag of nerves. She had never been to a grand occasion before and the thought of all those generals and admirals with their ladies gave her butterflies in her tummy. She had spent hours looking for something to wear and finally arrived home with a hour to spare still flustered and not quite satisfied with the new dress that she had purchased.

Ralph was already dressed in a brand new evening suit and looked very gallant but he wasn't looking forward to the grand occasion either.

"I've seen enough generals to last me a lifetime!" he thought, sitting by the fire, sipping a glass of sherry.

"I wonder what this commander is like?" he mused. "I'll bet he's one of the old school, fat through sitting behind a desk and never been to sea in his life. One of the old school-tie 'Pater bought him the commission' types..." He had seen enough of those as well: the damned army was full of them.

"Oh hell," he said to himself, feeling thoroughly depressed, "It's going to be awful!"

It was ten minutes to six when Helen came into the room and she looked magnificent. Ralph's mouth dropped open at the sight of her. She was wearing a bottle green gown made from heavy silk. It had an off-the-shoulder top and a large sash that encircled her narrow waist and tied in a big bow at her back.

"Well, Mr Grant, will I do to meet all the fine generals?" she asked laughingly.

"You look wonderful!" he gasped in reply. Suddenly the thought of a dreary evening was swept from his mind.

"No-one could match her beauty," he thought.

"I shall be the proudest man there!" he said, giving her a kiss.

Promptly at six o' clock there was a knock at the door. Mrs Coolridge entered the room followed by a smart-looking naval officer.

"Commander Mills is here," she announced. "Six o'clock prompt, just as he promised."

He was a man in his early thirties, five feet ten inches tall with dark hair and deep brown eyes which looked out from a weather-beaten face. He looked a strong rugged type and this was confirmed by his strong grip when he shook hands with Ralph at their introduction.

"My wife is waiting in the car," said the commander, "so if you and Miss Graham are ready I'd appreciate an early start, it's quite a way to Aylesbury."

Ralph liked him immediately he was a man's man. He did not bat an eyelid when he saw Ralph's face and his strong warm handshake gave Ralph the impression that they could be good friends.

On the way down to the car Ralph noticed that the commander had a limp and found it difficult to get into the car.

"Would you like me to drive?" asked Ralph, holding open the door for Helen.

"Would you?" replied the Commander in relief. "It's a hell of a long way to drive with a gammy leg. I'd be most grateful."

Helen and the Commander's wife, whose name was Kitty, sat in the back. Kitty was about the same age as Helen. She was small and blonde. Her hair was straight and cut short just below her ears. She had a pleasing roundish face and big blue eyes. She was a giggler and before long Helen and Kitty were having fits of laughter on the back seat.

They hadn't reached the end of Wellington Street before the Commander insisted that they all called each other by their first names.

“As far as I am concerned,” he said, “The bloody war is over and so is my career in the Navy. No more ‘Commander’, just plain Reg Mills. Sounds wonderful doesn’t it?”

Their journey had taken them through Aylesbury where they turned left at Whitchurch to a place called Pitchcott. The old hall was situated somewhere in the district but where they didn’t know. It was a cold night, the sky was clear and a bright full moon beamed down, lighting their way.

The roads were very narrow. Ralph slowed down, for the twists and turns in the country road were becoming hazardous as the surface began to freeze over.

He had just manoeuvred round a dangerous corner when a shimmering light suddenly rose from the road in front of them, not twenty feet away.

“What the hell is that?” shouted Reg Mills.

“God almighty!” cried Ralph, trying desperately to keep the car under control.

The women in the back screamed as the car veered first one way then another. The shimmering light towered high above them and no matter what Ralph did with the car, the dancing light was always in front.

“Stop the car, Ralph!” screamed Helen from the back.

Suddenly the light moved away further up the road. Ralph managed to bring the car down to a crawl, and safety.

“What is that thing?” Kitty called out.

“God knows!” replied Reg.

“Do you think we had better stop?” he asked Ralph.

“If I stop now,” Ralph called back, “I might never get going again. The best thing I can do is to go along slowly. It might disappear or something.”

They had travelled about half a mile, the strange light always keeping the same distance away. As they turned one of the many bends the light stopped moving. It rose about thirty feet into the night air and hovered there for a few seconds, then suddenly disappeared from sight.

“It’s gone!” Reg said quietly.

The four of them looked around to see if it would reappear. There was a deathly silence for several minutes. Then Ralph called out.

“Look there, up the road, a brazier and two Tommies standing by it, I’ll bet a week’s wages that’s the place were looking for.”

"I think you're right," replied Reg. "Look, there's a sign."

As Ralph drove up the road towards the Tommies he read the sign: "Bamford Manor War Department". He didn't take it in for a few seconds then it hit him.

"Bamford Manor, Good God! It can't be, not down here in the south!"

No one was listening to him they were all concerned with the Tommies and the directions they were giving.

"Carry on up the drive, sir," one was saying. "The big house is about half a mile further on. You can't miss it, there are braziers all the way."

"Straight on, Ralph," Reg said, turning to him.

Ralph just nodded. He couldn't believe it but he knew it was true. The light had guided them here and he fumbled for his crucifix beneath his shirt. He gave a sigh of relief as he felt the cross touch his hand.

"Are you all right?" Reg said softly so that the women couldn't hear.

"Er, yes, I'm fine…" replied Ralph, a little hesitantly. "Be damned glad to get a drink though."

"Won't be long now," laughed Reg.

"We're here," he said as they pulled up in front of a large flight of marble steps that led up to a very impressive main entrance guarded by four soldiers in dress uniform.

The whole place was alight and music could be heard coming from inside.

The sound of people laughing and calling to each other made the two women excited.

"Oh let's hurry, please," called Kitty to Reg. "I can't wait to get inside."

"Yes, come on Ralph," added Helen. "It sounds wonderful."

Ralph left the car for an attendant to move and followed them up to the main entrance where invitations were shown to a full-dress sergeant major. He was still thinking about the light and the name of the manor.

"Damned funny, that light thing in the road," Reg said, talking a drink from a waiter. "I wonder what it was?"

"Most probably something to do with the weather conditions," replied Ralph. "You know, frost, moon, that sort of thing."

"I suppose you're right," said Reg, finding somewhere to sit.

"This will do for me," he laughed. "Plenty to eat and drink and a place to put my gammy leg for the night."

Ralph had to laugh. The two women were overawed at the splendour of the place. The marble steps outside carried on up a grand staircase in the main hall; a stupendous chandelier hung from a magnificent ornamental ceiling. The place was crowded. Helen and Kitty had never seen such splendour. The uniforms of the officers and the gowns of their ladies were indescribable. The two could only stand and stare in amazement.

Upstairs was the ballroom. A military band was playing a waltz as Ralph and Helen took the floor together with the happy band of revellers. He couldn't get the light and the name of the place out of his mind, and it must have shown on his face.

"What's the matter?" Helen asked him as they danced. "Don't tell me there's nothing wrong, I know you too well for that. Is it that light on the road and the name of this place?"

"You connected the two as well, did you?" replied Ralph "It's too much of a coincidence. We were guided here by that light, I'm convinced of that. Do you have your crucifix with you? We can't be too careful!"

Helen nodded at his question.

"You won't let it spoil everything?" she asked pleadingly "I have so looked forward to it."

"Why no!" he called out loud and he laughed as he swung her round and round until she was quite dizzy.

It was about eleven thirty that Ralph and Helen went out onto the balcony for a breath of fresh air. They had danced the night away. She was exuberant never had she felt so wonderful.

"Oh, I never want it to stop!" she cried waltzing around on her own.

Ralph was looking at the back of the building.

"That's funny," he said leaning over the balcony to see properly.

"What is?" she replied, still dancing round.

"Come here a moment and look at this," he said mysteriously.

Helen went over and stood by his side.

"The rest of the house is in complete darkness," he said. "It looks as though it is in ruins,"

"Maybe it is," Helen replied, seemingly not interested, and she carried on with her dancing.

Ralph was still transfixed, staring into the blackness behind. Suddenly he called to her.

"My God, Helen, look at this!" he called, pointing upwards towards the roof.

Helen came running over to see. Whatever it was that Ralph had seen had gone.

"You're playing games with me," she laughed. "There's nothing there."

"I swear there was something there," he replied, excitedly. "Up on the roof, it was a glow of light."

As she stood there, looking up to where he was pointing, an eerie glow appeared from behind the facade. It shone for a few moments then disappeared. They looked at each other in silence as though waiting, each for the other to speak. It was Ralph that broke the uneasy quiet.

"Well, shall I say it or will you?" he said, turning back to look at the roof.

"It could be anyone or anything up there," "she replied, not wanting to believe what he meant.

Ralph did not reply. His eyes were fixed on the spot where the glow had been. Suddenly it was there again, but this time in a window on the top floor. They watched until it disappeared again.

"I don't like it!" Helen cried, running off into the ballroom.

Ralph was just going to follow her when the glow appeared again. This time it was only a few yards away from the lights of the ballroom.

"My God, she's coming here!" he cried and he dashed in panic into the midst of the revellers.

'Which way to go? Where was Helen? Got to get out of here…'

His mind was in a turmoil as he dashed through the crowded ballroom. He was just about to rush down the stairs when a voice called out.

"Hey, Ralph, where are you off to in such a hurry?"

He turned to see Reg Mills waving at him.

"Come over here, old chap," he called "There's someone I want you to meet."

Before he knew what had happened Reg Mills had come over to him and taken hold of his arm. He was drunk.

"You must meet this beautiful friend of mine" he blurted, pushing his way through the crowd. "She's the most beautiful thing you've ever seen and that's a fact."

There was a crowd of young officers gathered around someone, all talking and laughing. Some were drunk and showing off to whoever it was they were talking to. Ralph tried to pull away, explaining bitterly that he was looking for Helen. But it was to no avail: drunk or not the grip of Reg Mills was like iron. The crowd parted as Reg pushed his way through some of them, objecting strongly at being shoved to one side. As they reached the centre of attraction that was sending all these young men crazy, Reg stopped and in triumph held out his hand to Ralph saying:

"Now what do you think of that?" and he staggered a little as he held on to Ralph.

Standing with her back to them, was a woman with long flowing blonde hair that reached down to her waist. She was wearing a long white dress that touched the floor. The woman was busily talking to some young officers.

"Jennie!" Reg called out. "This is the friend I wanted you to meet."

Ralph stared at the long blonde hair and the white dress. He was petrified but he wanted to see her face. It was as though he was compelled by some inner longing to see the woman of his dreams again.

The woman turned to see who was calling her. She was still laughing at something somebody had said to her. She was just as Reg had said but more. Only in his dreams had he seen such perfection. The face seemed different somehow. It wasn't the same as he remembered from his dreams but there was a resemblance. It wasn't in the features, it was the eyes. They were the same deep blue eyes that seemed to penetrate into a man's inner soul. The same deep pools of blue that could send a man stark raving mad for her.

"Ah Reg, you're back with your friend!" she said, looking at Ralph and smiling.

Ralph moved back a pace. He could do nothing but stare at her. The voice, that wonderful seductive voice, was the same and the smile, oh, how he remembered that smile.

"Come on, man!" laughed Reg. "She won't eat you!"

Then he turned to the woman and said: "This is my friend of four hours, or is it longer, I forget. I'm a little drunk... Anyway this is Ralph Grant."

Then he turned to Ralph who was still staring and introduced the goddess that stood before him.

"Ralph old man, this is Mrs Ryan."

She held out her hand to him. He just stood there stupefied, looking first at the hand and then at her. She was smiling and saying something but he wasn't listening. He was remembering all the terrible things that had happened over the last month or so. Suddenly a hand was pressed into his and he was startled back to reality.

"Ralph, where have you been?" a voice was saying. It was Helen standing close to him. She looked at his face and then at the woman, and she didn't like what she saw. Jealousy reared its ugly head. She had no idea what was going on in his mind. All she could see was a beautiful woman holding out her hand to her Ralph and giving him a seductive look.

"Ralph" she repeated, "it's nearly twelve o'clock" and she pulled at his arm, dragging him backwards away from the beautiful Jennie Ryan and her admirers.

As she pulled him along she heard Reg call out "That is jealousy for you!" and the whole group roared with laughter.

She was now humiliated, furious and jealous. All that she wanted to do was to get as far away from everybody as she could. Leaving Ralph standing there she ran off down the great marble staircase. Ralph, who had regained his composure, shouted after her but she was in such a state that she did not respond to his pleas. He kept her in sight as he followed her, being as polite as possible as he knocked into people on the way. Helen had run down a passage that led from the main entrance. When Ralph reached it there was no sign of her. He slowly walked along trying each door that he came to but they were all locked. At the far end of the passage the lights were out and as he approached the shadows he could hear sobbing.

"Helen!" he called softly.

"Go away!" came the reply between the sobs.

He found her behind a pillar hiding in the darkness.

"Whatever is the matter?" he said, taking her in his arms.

"I want to go home," she sobbed "It's all been spoilt by Reg Mills and that woman you were staring at."

"I've got something to tell you about her," he replied. "She is not what she seems. Let us find somewhere quiet so that we can talk."

Just then they heard the band playing Auld Lang Syne. Ralph held her close and kissed her.

"Happy New Year, darling" he said softly.

"Happy New Year, my love," she replied, tears still streaming down her face.

"Let's get out of this mayhem," he said as the revellers came screaming down the passage towards them, all throwing streamers, wearing paper hats and seemingly very drunk.

Ralph ran deeper into the shadows pulling Helen behind him. They were running along a wide corridor. There were windows to their left that let in the moonlight. At the end of the corridor they had to stop. In front of them, barring their way, was a large double door.

"Now what do we do?" asked Helen.

"We do this," replied Ralph, reaching for the doorknob.

"We can't just open it and go in!" she said, grabbing his hand. "It must be private, the owner might not like it. Then what would we do?"

"If there's any one in there I'll apologise for the intrusion," he whispered in her ear and without more ado he opened the door.

The room was in darkness except for the glow from the fire burning in a large open fireplace. They went inside, closing the door behind them. Helen gripped Ralph's hand and stood close up to him as they surveyed their surroundings. The room looked like a palace, luxurious in every respect. Never had they seen such richness.

"Let's get out of here!" whispered Helen. "Someone might come in."

Ralph was thinking the same thing when he noticed a large picture hanging above the fireplace.

"Good God," he whispered. "Look at that!" and he slowly walked over to have a closer look. Helen followed, still clinging on to him and looking around her all the time, fully expecting someone to come into the room.

As they neared the painting, Helen looked at it for the first time.

"Good Heavens!" she whispered in horror. "It's the woman you were staring at in the ballroom."

Ralph did not say a word but went over and read a plaque at the base of the portrait.

Suddenly everything became clear to him.

"Well, I'll be damned!" he said, coming over to her. "Of course that's it,why didn't I think of it before?"

"Think of what?" Helen whispered, looking around more frightened than before. "Please let's get out of here!" she pleaded.

"You're right!" he said making a move towards the door. "This is no place for us."

Once outside they walked quickly down the corridor and joined the merry throng. All the time Helen was pestering him to tell her what he had found out.

"Later!" he replied. "Let's get away from here first. We've got to find Reg Mills and Kitty."

They had to fight their way through crowds of drunken officers who tried to insist on kissing Helen but Ralph was having none of it and shoved them aside in no uncertain manner.

They eventually found Reg Mills sprawled out at the bottom of the marble staircase, blind drunk. Poor Kitty was sitting beside him looking very upset.

"Oh, where have you been?" she cried when she saw them "Just look at him, isn't it disgusting? I've been harassed and propositioned by drunken louts calling themselves officers. This is an orgy not a party! Please take me home."

"That's just what were going to do," Ralph said, pulling Reg up and throwing him over his shoulder like a rag doll.

"Try to find out where the car is!" he called to them as he picked his way past dozens of drunken couples cavorting on the floor.

The girls had done a good job of finding the car and by the time he had manoeuvred his way down the marble steps at the front it was waiting there with the engine running.

An army corporal was standing there with the back door open waiting to help with the drunken Reg. A good tip and their wishes for a happy New Year was all that was needed to send them on their way, but as Ralph was getting into the car he took a backwards look at the old house. There standing at the head of the marble steps was the woman with the long blonde hair looking down at them.

Ralph wouldn't tell Helen what he suspected while Kitty was listening. She was furious with him but she understood. It wasn't until Kitty was fast asleep on the back seat along side the snoring Reg that Ralph began to explain.

"Do you remember me telling you that it was a Major Ryan who offered me the cottage and when he died his wife kept his promise?"

"Yes," replied Helen impatiently. "Go on."

"Well, I'm convinced that the woman at the Manor House is the Major's wife."

"You don't mean it!" Helen replied in disbelief.

"But that's not all," he carried on. "You thought that the woman in the portrait was her, didn't you?"

"Well, it was, wasn't it?" Helen answered.

"Not so," replied Ralph. "The woman in the portrait was Lady Mary Bamford, the witch who was burnt at the stake in the seventeenth century. The very same being that has caused me all my terrors since I first went to that damned cottage."

"My God!" cried Helen. "Then this Mrs Ryan is a direct descendant of hers, she even looks like her. She couldn't be one and the same could she? Oh, my God, that's just too terrible to think of!"

"I don't think she is," he replied.

"But we will have to be very careful who we make friends with," he carried on and looking towards the back seat, added pointedly "He knew her as a good friend and it was he who came to bring us to the Manor."

"That's right," Helen said turning round to look at Reg Mills. "But he doesn't look the type to be involved with anything like witchcraft ."

"That's the trouble," Ralph replied. "They never do."

CHAPTER EIGHT

It was now three weeks into the New Year and 1919 had come with a vengeance. Heavy snow had fallen all over the country and London had more than its share. Londoners had awakened to find their streets blocked by three feet of snow. The city was like a ghost town and nothing could move. Huge gangs of men were sent out to clear the streets so that essential food, bread, milk, meat and potatoes, could get to the shops.

Hardly anyone was working. It was virtually impossible unless a person worked locally to get across the town. This was the situation that Ralph and Helen found themselves in although he had been out helping local volunteers to clear the neighbourhood.

On the evening of the second day after the snowfall Ralph had arrived back at Number 32 exhausted. He had been out since early morning helping to shovel tons of wet snow into the river.

"A hot bath and a good hot meal, that's what you want, Mr Ralph," Mrs Coolridge said as she saw him coming up the front steps to the house.

"I don't think I've got the energy for either!" laughed Ralph pulling off his big boots. "I've never worked so hard in all my life and I don't want to see another spade as long as I live."

But two hours later, after having his bath and meal, Ralph and Helen were sitting by the fire sipping their evening glasses of sherry. After the hard day's work out in the cold Ralph was feeling tired and the bath followed by a good meal and the heat from the fire was sending him to sleep.

Helen watched him as his eyelids began to droop and his head began to roll from side to side.

"Come on my lad," she whispered softly in his ear. "It's time you were in bed."

Ralph muttered an unintelligible reply as he stood up and walked in a dream to the door.

"Good night, darling," Helen called after him. "Sweet dreams!"

She heard a grunt as he closed the door behind him and she giggled to herself, saying: "Poor lamb!"

He was asleep almost before his head had touched the pillow. It was in the early hours that he awoke with a start. He had been having a bad dream and sweat was pouring from him. Lying there trying to collect his thoughts he noticed how quiet it was, and he also noticed that he hadn't drawn the curtains. The gas lights from the street shone through the window, casting strange shadows over the room.

Ralph turned onto his side as sleep began to overtake him once again, but a strange sound that seemed to come from inside the room had him wide awake. He lay there, too frightened to move, his eyes scanning the darkest corners. It came again, a growling sort of noise as though an animal was in the room. He felt for his crucifix and to his horror he found that he had left it off after his bath.

"It's over on the dressing table!" he thought. "What am I going to do?"

The noise became louder and he could see something moving at the side of the large wardrobe.

"What the hell is it?" he thought, as he slipped under the blankets to the other side of the bed, away from the intruder.

Suddenly the thing in the shadows came out into the shaft of light that was coming in through the window. By this time Ralph was on his knees at the side of the bed, staring at it.

"Good God, it's Sittwell!" he said in disbelief and he kept low at the side of the bed out of sight, watching him.

Sittwell didn't seem to know what he was doing. He looked mad and he was banging into things, snarling like a wild animal at the shafts of light.

Ralph crawled towards the dressing table and as he reached up for the crucifix Sittwell saw him. He roared like a demented beast and flung himself at Ralph who managed to roll away at the last minute, leaving Sittwell to go smashing into the dressing table, scattering all before him and ending up on the floor.

Seeing his chance, Ralph dashed to the door but it appeared to be locked. As he struggled to open it the crazy Sittwell was up again and coming for him, screaming and frothing at the mouth. Ralph tried to get away but two strong hands gripped him from behind and hurled him into the wardrobe, smashing the long mirror in the door. Ralph was cut and dazed. Sittwell grabbed him again and flung him over the bed onto the floor.

Suddenly there was banging on the bedroom door and screaming from Helen and Mrs Coolridge.

Sittwell launched himself again at Ralph, biteing, scratching, clawing at everything in sight. Ralph threw bedclothes over him but to no avail, he just kept on coming. Within minutes the room was in a shambles.

Ralph was eventually cornered near the window and as Sittwell threw himself at him once again he picked up one of the bowls of holy water that he had placed on the windowsill and flung it into Sittwell's face.

There was an almighty scream from him and he clawed at his face as though he was blinded or burnt, but in his madness he still rushed forward and he crashed headlong through the window into the street below.

Ralph pulled himself up from the floor, still dazed from the incessant attacks. The women were still screaming outside on the landing and banging on the door. He leaned over and looked through the smashed window but he pulled back in horror at what he saw. Sittwell was impaled on the railings at the front of the house.

"Ralph, my God, Ralph, open the door!" he heard Helen screaming from outside. Slowly he made his way to the door which now opened easily and he passed out in her arms.

Two hours later he heard voices, whispering voices, and as he opened his eyes he saw Inspector Sharp looking down at him.

"Well, young fella," he said, "it was nearly you this time, wasn't it?"

Ralph didn't reply, he just looked around.

"Where's Helen?" he asked.

"Oh, she's fine," replied the Inspector. "She's making a drink for you, something that will buck you up. Well then, now that you're awake what can you tell me about it? All that I can see is a smashed-up room, a broken window and some dirty clothes hanging over the railings outside."

Ralph looked at him in amazement.

"What do you mean, 'dirty clothes'?" he said, sitting up. "Where's the body?"

"Body? What body?" replied Inspector Sharp, looking puzzled "We haven't found a body."

"But he was impaled on the railings!" cried Ralph. "I saw him with my own eyes! I saw him…"

"There's nothing on the railings but a pile of old clothes," replied the Inspector quietly, trying not to get Ralph too upset. "And there's not a trace of blood on them either."

"I don't believe this," said Ralph, getting impatient. "I could have been killed up there in that room. Sittwell was like a raging bull, a wild animal, he was frothing at the mouth!"

"Sittwell?" butted in the Inspector. "William Sittwell was in your room?"

"That's what I'm trying to tell you," Ralph cried, standing up and walking about, feeling very frustrated.

"He somehow or other appeared there I don't know how, he just did."

"And it was he who smashed up the room?" asked the Inspector.

"For God's sake, man!" shouted Ralph. "That's what I'm telling you!"

"I find all this very confusing," replied Inspector Sharp. "I know there must have been a terrible fight because your Miss Helen and Mrs Coolridge confirmed it. What I want to know is where has the body gone to? It just can't disappear into thin air."

"Maybe Sittwell wasn't there at all?" said Ralph sarcastically. "Maybe I just imagined the whole bloody thing like the last time in the attic room, when Lomas's head went missing. Maybe you imagined that, Inspector."

"It's no use getting upset," the Inspector replied, quietly. "I realise what you've been through couldn't have been pleasant but we'll get nowhere arguing with each other. Now come and sit down and start at the beginning."

It was daylight when Inspector Sharp left Number 32 Wellington Street still bewildered at what had happened and he gave no indication that he would return. As he had told Ralph before he left, he was only mortal, only a higher being could solve this case.

It wasn't only the traumatic experience that Ralph had to deal with. Mrs Coolridge had been very quiet since that terrible night and a few days later she invited Ralph into her sitting room for a talk.

"I don't like doing this," she said, sitting there strait-laced and looking the complete landlady that she was. "But after all that has happened since you arrived in my house I have no alternative but to ask you to leave. I feel very sorry for you and Miss Helen. Of course she doesn't have to go, but I expect you to be out of your room by the week-end."

Ralph could understand her feelings and said that he would comply with her wishes, but he didn't want her to tell Helen just yet. Mrs Coolridge agreed to his request on condition that he never came near her house again.

Two days later Ralph had found himself a room in a small boarding house alongside the river. It was a bit rough but the linen was clean and it would do until he could find somewhere better.

When he eventually told Helen about the move she was very upset and wanted to ask Mrs Coolridge to change her mind. But Ralph would hear none of it. He told her that he had decided that it was for the best. She would be safer with him living away from Wellington Street. It was him the supernatural being wanted and by moving away he would draw it away from her.

It was early March and Ralph had settled down in his new surroundings. Nothing had happened since that dreadful night and everything seemed to be returning to normal. They had taken to eating out a lot while they were living apart and one evening after work Ralph took Helen to their favourite café in the West End. As they were waiting to be served Ralph was reading the evening paper when he suddenly said:

"Good God, Helen, look at this!" and he passed the paper over to her, indicating the place he had just read.

"Cottage to rent," she read aloud. "Suit young man, quiet country village, nearby fishing. Apply Bamford Manor, Pitchcott near Whitchurch, Aylesbury."

Her eyes were wide in astonishment before she had finished.

"You don't think it's the same thing over again, do you?" she gasped.

"What else can I think?" he replied, his eyes narrowing in thought. "I've a good mind to reply to that advertisement and finish this thing once and for all."

"Oh no, Ralph!" she cried out. "You mustn't do it, you could end up like Sittwell."

People were looking at them. A waiter came across to see what was wrong.

"Nothing wrong!" Ralph said, feeling embarrassed. "Just a friendly discussion, you know how it is?"

The waiter smiled and winked at Ralph in a knowing way then went on with his work. The rest of the diners carried on with their own business, leaving Helen furious at having gained their attention in the first place.

"I'm sorry for shouting," she whispered across the table. "But please don't do it, Ralph. You don't know what could happen to you. I might never see you again if you go to that place."

Ralph looked at the anguish that was showing on her lovely face and he reached out and clasped her hand in his.

"Don't worry, love," he whispered, gently squeezing her hand. "I wouldn't do anything silly. Don't forget I know what it's like to be in her clutches. I must be the only one to have escaped from her and she doesn't like it. That's why I'm having all this trouble, and I've got to stop it somehow or other or it will be with us for the rest of our lives."

"Maybe this is a trap to get you there," she said, looking at the paper. "She will do anything, you know that."

Ralph thought for a while as he gazed into her troubled eyes.

"I've got it!" he said excitedly. "I'll book a room at that inn, the one we passed not far from the Manor. What was it called?"

"'The Raven,'" Helen replied. "And don't you mean we will book a room?" she added, determinedly staring him straight in the eyes.

There was silence for a few moments as her answer, which had thrown him off balance for a moment, sank in.

"I don't like it," he replied. "You could be in great danger. I couldn't live with myself if anything happened to you."

"Now you know how I feel!" she said, sitting upright in her chair and folding her arms in her own stubborn way.

He looked at her and then a grin covered his face.

"All right," he laughed. "If we've got to go, we'll go together!"

She was going to jump up and kiss him but she looked around and changed her mind. Instead she grunted her approval and began to eat her meal that the waiter had just served.

It was a week later that Ralph and Helen set off in an old staff car that he had purchased from surplus stocks at the War Office. Spring was on the way, and although it was cold the sun was shining, giving them a holiday feeling as they drove along the country lanes.

They arrived at The Raven Inn about two hours later, the car having had to have minor repairs along the way. It was an eighteenth century coach-house and it was nearer than they had expected to the Manor which they could see across the fields. The inn was built out of the same stone as the Manor and gave the impression that it used to be a lodge that belonged to the big house.

The interior of the inn was spick and span although it still retained its atmosphere of days gone by. The furnishings and the decor looked original and well preserved as though the place had only just opened.

Mine host of the hostelry didn't fit the surroundings. He was a thin miserable-looking man in his fifties: small and sickly-looking. His hair was receding and seemed to be falling out in places. His face resembled a rodent of sorts. He had small slitty eyes, a large nose, slightly prominent teeth and large ears that stuck out from his head.

He didn't seem pleased to see them as they signed the register. And Master Graylish, as the servant girl called him, laid the law down in no uncertain manner.

"Breakfast at seven, no lunch, dinner at seven thirty, no supper and The Raven closes at eleven o'clock every night. Locked, bolted and barred whether you're in or out, it doesn't make any difference to me. Do you understand?" he said in a sneering voice.

Ralph and Helen looked at each other as they were taken up to their respective rooms.

"Charming fellow!" Helen said as they reached the top of the stairs and started to follow the young girl who was carrying their bags. When the trio reached the end of the passage the girl stopped outside a door.

"This be your room, Master," she said to Ralph.

He opened the door and fully expected her to bring his case in. But she froze, her eyes staring into the room as though she was expecting to see something terrible inside.

"Is there something wrong, miss?" he asked her.

"N-n-no, Master," she stuttered, still staring into the room, then she pushed a key into Helen's hand, pointed at the door opposite to Ralph's and cried out "That one's yours, Miss!" and she ran off down the passage.

"What a strange carry-on," Helen said, looking at Ralph.

Ralph, who by this time was inside his room, turned to look around.

"Well, I'll be damned!" he gasped.

"Just look at this!" he said, beckoning to Helen who came and stood by his side.

"Oh, my God!" she cried as she saw the object he was pointing to.

Over the fireplace was a portrait of The Lady Of The Manor.

“That’s coming down while I’m in here,” he said, going over to it and lifting it from its hook on the wall.

“Something must have happened in this room to make that poor girl so frightened,” Helen said, looking about her. “I wonder what it was?”

“It could have been anything, after seeing that picture,” he replied.

“Come on,” he said, going out into the passage. “Let’s see what your room’s like.”

They opened the door and looked inside. What they saw they couldn’t believe.

“It’s just the same as yours!” Helen gasped as she walked around the room. “Everything is just the same. Curtains, carpet, bedding, picture, everything.”

“And the shape of the room is the same,” agreed Ralph. “Each room is a replica of the other. How strange.”

“There’s something funny going on here,” Helen said. “I don’t like it. I think we should get out before something happens to us.”

“I’m not leaving,” Ralph replied. “No way am I leaving! I’m seeing this through to the bitter end no matter what the consequences might be and that’s final. If you want to leave I’ll drive you to the nearest railway station.”

“Oh, I didn’t mean I’d leave you!” she cried out, nearly in tears. “I wanted us both to leave this place. It frightens me.”

Ralph went over to her and put his arms around her.

“I know, love,” he said softly. “And I’m sorry for shouting like that but now that we’re here we might as well see what happens, at least for one night.”

Helen looked up at him and smiled.

“All right,” she agreed. “Just for one night” and she kissed him and held him tight as though for reassurance.

“Now let’s get settled in,” he said, holding her at arms length.

“This wants removing for a start,” he said, going over to the picture and taking it down from the wall. “The less I see of her the better I’ll feel.”

“Where are you going to put it?” asked Helen looking a little worried. “What if someone should come in and notice it missing?”

Ralph looked around for a suitable hiding-place and going over to the large cupboard in the corner of the room he opened the door.

"Here we are," he said. "Just the place, and there's a key to lock it as well. That's all the better, we can take the key with us."

He placed the picture inside and locked the cupboard door.

"There we are," he said feeling proud of himself and holding up the key to Helen. "And I'll do the same thing in my room. That's a good start, isn't it?" he laughed.

Helen gave him a worried smile in return but she was far from happy with her surroundings.

"Can't we stay together for tonight?" she pleaded "I'm frightened to be left alone. No-one will know and anyhow I don't care if they do. Please, Ralph, I want to be with you."

The outburst came as a surprise to him. He hadn't realised how frightened she was and he went over to her, encircling her in his strong arms.

"Maybe you're right," he said softly. "Two heads are better than one and if anything does happen we could fight it together."

They decided to stay in Helen's room. They reasoned that the landlord knew which room Ralph was in and that if there was any trouble it would come in that room, also that was the room which the maid wouldn't enter.

It was seven thirty as Ralph and Helen came down the staircase and made their way towards the dining room. Something seemed wrong. When they had arrived at the inn there were lots of people and they assumed that the place was full. But as they entered the dining room they stood and stared in amazement. The room was empty. Every table was bare except for one small table in the centre and at the side of the table stood a waitress. When she saw them she solemnly held out her hand towards the table inviting them to take their seats.

They looked at each other and Helen gripped Ralph's hand tightly.

"What shall we do?" she asked through gritted teeth.

"We will take our places," he replied "I'm starving, aren't you?"

They walked slowly towards the waitress and sat down. The woman did not say a word she did not offer them a menu or tell them what there was for dinner. She just turned and walked away.

The atmosphere was eerie not a sound could be heard. It seemed as though they were the only people in the whole place. Helen looked around at the empty room.

"Where are all the people?" she whispered across the table to Ralph.

"I don't know," he replied in the same vein. "But it's certainly very, very strange. I don't like it at all."

A few moments later the waitress came in carrying a large tray which she set down on an empty table close by. Ralph and Helen looked at each other in expectation. The woman came over and placed two bowls of soup in front of them, then she retired to the empty table and stood there watching them. As soon as they had finished with the soup she quickly came over and served them with a cold chicken salad, once again retiring to the empty table, this time sitting on one of the vacant chairs.

"I don't believe this," Ralph whispered to Helen. "I have never felt so unwanted in all my life."

Helen sneaked a quick look at the waitress.

"She's rapping her fingers on the table," she whispered back at Ralph. "Do you think she's in a hurry?" and she started to giggle.

Ralph could see the funny side of the situation and joined in the giggling. It took no time at all before they were laughing at the tops of their voices. Every time they looked at the waitress they would roar out in fits of laughter until they could stand it no longer and they left the dining room holding on to each other, laughing with tears rolling down their faces.

It was a good half hour before they had calmed down but their spirits were still high as they made their way back to the room upstairs.

"It's no good just sitting here looking at each other," Ralph said jumping up from the bed. "We should be doing something."

"Like what?" asked Helen with a twinkle in her eye.

"Like going out and exploring…" he replied, ignoring her naughty twinkle. "We should be finding out about the place. You know, getting the feel of it."

"Exactly how I feel," laughed Helen as she threw her arms around his neck. "I know something exciting we could do."

"You know what I mean!" said Ralph, blushing and trying to pull her arms away. "There's a time and a place for everything and right now we should be out there trying to find out what goes on around here."

"You're a spoil-sport, Ralph Grant!" Helen said as she taunted him by pulling his shirt front from his trousers.

"We've come here for a purpose," he said, getting annoyed. But before he could say any more she kissed him passionately.

As they were locked in each other's arms a strange noise came from the corner of the room. They froze and still with their lips pressed tightly together they opened their eyes and stared at each other in trepidation.

"What was that?" Helen whispered.

Ralph put his finger to his lips and motioning to her to stay where she was he moved slowly towards the cupboard in the corner. He felt beneath his shirt for the gold crucifix and at the same time produced the cupboard key from his pocket. Standing with the key at the ready he tried to regain his composure but his hand shook as he inserted it in the lock. Taking a deep breath he quickly turned it. The lock clicked open. Ralph slowly gripped the knob and after another deep breath he turned it and flung the door open, stepping well back as he did so.

"My God!" he gasped.

"What is it?" Helen cried from the other side of the room.

"It's the picture!" he replied in amazement. "Come and see!"

Helen moved slowly over to him, petrified at what she was about to see. Standing close behind him she peeped into the cupboard.

"Well, what about that?" he asked.

"It's impossible!" she eventually gasped in reply.

"Impossible or not, it's happened!" he said, taking a closer look at the picture. "I've told you anything can happen when this woman is involved."

"But how can she just disappear from a picture? It doesn't make sense," Helen said, still staring at the empty frame.

"I wonder…?" Ralph said, dashing to the bedroom door.

"Where are you going?" screamed Helen in terror, running after him. Ralph did not reply, he dashed out of the room across the corridor and into his room. Going to his cupboard he produced the picture that had hung on his wall. Helen was right behind him, looking about her all the time, expecting she knew not what.

"There!" he said holding up the picture-frame. "She's gone from this one, too."

"What does it all mean?" Helen said in a whisper, still looking around terrified at the slightest thing.

"I think it means that there's something big happening tonight," he replied as he sat on the bed.

"Like what?" she whispered.

"I don't know exactly," he answered, stroking his chin in deep thought. "But it's all beginning to fit together," he carried on. "The Inn was full of people when we arrived, now they have all disappeared. And that fiasco at dinner, that waitress wanted us out of the way as though she was in a hurry to go somewhere. Now this..." he said, looking at the picture frame.

"There must be some sort of meeting up at the Old House, that's what it is!" he said excitedly and he stood up, his eyes shining with determination.

"Come on, this is our chance to finish it once and for all."

CHAPTER NINE

Wrapped up warm to keep out the cold night air, they set off leaving the empty inn behind them. It was a clear night, a full moon lit up the surrounding countryside making their expedition into unknown territory easier going. It wasn't long before they had reached a high wall that was covered with creeper.

"This must be the perimeter wall," Ralph whispered. "Come on, we'll follow it round to the back of the house there must be a way in somewhere."

Helen wasn't too sure they were doing the right thing but she didn't dare say anything to him, not in his present mood. He was determined to end the nightmare one way or another.

Ralph pressed on along the edge of the wall. The undergrowth was becoming thicker and Helen's long skirt was being ripped to shreds by the briars and brambles that encircled them.

"Oh Ralph," she hissed at him. "I can't go on like this, isn't there some easier way to get in?"

"Won't be long now," he whispered back to her, then "Ah! here we go!" as he came across a crumbled section of wall.

"I told you we would find somewhere," he said in triumph, helping her to climb over the fallen stones.

Once inside the grounds Ralph moved slowly forward. Helen grabbed hold of his hand saying "Don't you dare go on without me. I'm sticking by you no matter what happens, do you hear me?"

"If you're not quiet, everybody will hear you," he hissed back in reply.

The undergrowth inside was no different from that of the outside. The whole place was overgrown, it was just like a jungle. They were making their way through a clump of trees when a horrific screech rent the air, not more than ten feet away from them. Helen screamed and flung herself at Ralph. He too was scared and for a moment was off balance. They both tumbled to the ground.

"What was it?" she cried as she scrambled to get close to him for protection.

"I don't know," he whispered in reply. "Just lie here for a moment or two and listen."

The cry came again and this time it was more like a baby. Then a squeaking noise could be heard.

"It's a rabbit," he chuckled. "A weasel or some other predator has caught it."

"Oh, how awful!" she cried, burying her head under his arm.

"Now come on, love," he said pulling her close to him "You'll have to be more brave than that! Things will get a lot worse before this night is out."

Ralph gave her a few minutes to calm down and wished now that he hadn't brought her. It would be hard enough to cope with the unknown ahead of him, let alone having to look after her as well. After a suitable time they were on their way again, threading their path to the edge of the small wood.

Standing in the shadows of the trees they stopped and Ralph pointed ahead. In front of them was the huge black mass of the Manor House. The moon was directly behind the house, producing a gigantic silhouette. Everywhere was quiet.

"That's strange!" he whispered "There's not a light to be seen anywhere. The place looks deserted."

"Maybe they have gone somewhere else," Helen said hopefully. "If there's nobody here there's not much point in staying, is there?"

"You must be joking!" he snapped back at her. "This is just the opportunity I've been waiting for. If there's nobody in the place I'm going to have a good snoop around while the going's good. If you don't want to come, wait here for me. I won't be long," and he started to move across the open space towards the house.

"Ralph!" she cried, running after him. "Don't you dare leave me alone."

As they neared and then were taken into the shadow of the great house Ralph stopped, and looking up at the towering edifice he said: "This must be the part of the house that's derelict. There are no windows, the stonework is crumbling and I can see the moon through the roof. Keep well back, Helen, there may be danger if we get too near any holes, that sort of thing. Come on, we'll make our way around to the front, the way we came on New Year's Eve."

Helen followed him closely and soon they were standing in front of the grand steps that rose to the front doors.

"There's something wrong here," Ralph said, going forward. "It wasn't like this the last time we came."

He walked slowly up the steps, there were stones and rubble everywhere. The great oak doors were hanging from their hinges and creaked as a breeze blew from inside the great house.

"What's happened to it?" Helen asked in amazement "It just couldn't go like this in a few months, something must have happened."

Ralph stood there looking at the old building, bewildered at what he was seeing. He sat down on the top step, looking about him and thinking.

After a while he suddenly sprang to his feet.

"That's it!" he said excitedly. "Why didn't I realise it before? What a fool I've been!"

"Realise what?" asked Helen, just as excited. "What is it?"

"Remember I told you about the cottage up in the Lake District and how it started to crumble after a while?" he said, walking about still thinking hard.

"Yes, I remember, what of it?" she replied getting agitated.

"Well, the same thing has happened here," he cried, pointing at the derelict house. "Don't you see if she isn't, to put it royally, 'in residence' the place reverts to its original state! That's what has happened all over, the village, the cottage and now here. Wherever she goes the place returns to its former splendour and when she leaves and has no further use for it, or has finished with her victim, the places fall into decay."

Helen stood looking at him for a moment. She was about to scoff at the idea but then she remembered how it was on New Year's Eve. The place had been alive with singing, happy people. The old house was beautiful, the grand marble staircase, the ballroom and the room they had entered with its wonderful furnishings, but how could this be, she wondered. She was about to ask Ralph the same question when a sound of voices came from out of the woods on the other side of the old house.

"Shh!" Ralph whispered, holding his finger to his lips.

The sound rang out again, it was a woman laughing. They stood looking at each other, frightened to move. It seemed like an eternity but the sound did not come again.

"I'll bet they're all in the woods," whispered Ralph. Then he paused, his eyes lighting up.

"Of course the cottage, they'll all be at the cottage, the one that was advertised in the paper. Come on, we've got to see what's going on."

This time Helen did not falter, she was fast believing that all he had told her was true. They entered the woods prepared for the worst. Ralph had stopped at the edge making sure that Helen wore her crucifix outside her top coat in full view of anyone or anything that she might come across. With a phial of Holy Water each, they carefully made their way through the trees stopping every time they heard a sound.

It seemed as though they had been there for hours, their progress was so slow. Ralph was beginning to wonder if they were going in the right direction when they heard the sound of people chanting not very far in front of them.

Ralph pulled Helen down behind a tree.

"Keep close behind me," he whispered to her. "Keep low and no matter what you see don't make a sound!" and he kissed her on the cheek.

Helen nodded in response and even though she was terrified, the kiss was reassuring to her.

Ralph pressed on towards the chanting which was starting to rise and fall. It sounded terrible, more like a lamentable wail. Suddenly there were lights ahead and sparks from a fire shooting up into the night sky. A few yards more and Ralph crouched low on the ground, motioning to Helen to come up beside him. As she did so Ralph parted the branches of a small bush. Helen's eyes opened wide at the scene that was set before them.

They were looking down into a great hole that was set out like an amphitheatre. Large pillars surrounded the pit, each carrying a flaming torch. At the far end a stone altar stood high on a pyramid of marble steps. Directly behind the altar and towering above the idolatrous congregation stood a large statue of human form with the head of a beast. The people nearest to them were wearing rough-looking monks' habits and there must have been fifty or sixty of them. Either side of the beast's statue and also looking down on the congregation were what seemed to be a hierarchy of priests, who wore white habits with long pointed hoods.

There was a strange silence among the worshippers as though they were expecting something to happen. Then from out of the darkness to the left of them came a slowly walking line of women each wearing a thin white robe. There were six of them, and slowly they made their way towards the altar.

Once they were in front of the altar they stopped and turned to face the beast's statue. Silence still reigned, it was eerie. Ralph and Helen looked at each other.

"It looks like some sort of initiation ceremony," he whispered.

As they looked again two men came from behind the great statue. They were naked to the waist. One of them was carrying a large head-dress made from the head of a bull. He was very tall and thin. When Ralph saw him he nearly cried out in horror and turning to Helen he pointed at the man.

"It's Sittwell!" he whispered hysterically, "The man in my room that night!"

Helen's eyes were staring and her mouth dropped open as she heard him but she was too horror-struck to reply.

They turned once again in trepidation, their eyes transfixed on the scene below.

Sittwell held the head-dress up high, showing it to the hooded congregation. A murmur of appreciation welled up from them. He placed the head-dress firmly on his partner's head. The man, who up to this time had looked quiet and somewhat in a trance, suddenly sprang to life in a wild fashion. It was as though the head of the beast had taken him over. He was bellowing and snorting like a bull as he leaped up onto the altar.

A stronger murmur came from the worshippers as one of the white robed women was brought forward and laid on the altar by two of the priests. All went quiet again. The man in the head-dress raised his arms to the statue and cried in a loud voice:

"Princess of darkness, Princess of our souls, we the Devil's spawn beseech thee, come to us, oh wonderful one!"

Everyone had their eyes fixed on the idol. Suddenly the ground shuddered and the whole congregation flung themselves prostrate before the hideous beast.

Helen grabbed tight hold of Ralph's arm saying fearfully: "What is it? what's going on?"

Ralph pulled her down behind the bush and put his hand over her mouth.

"Be quiet!" he hissed at her. "How do I know what it is? Just watch and see" and he parted the branches once again to survey the scene

What he saw made him start back.

"Jesus save us!" he cried, as he buried his head in his hands.

Helen pulled down the branch to see what had shocked him and crouched there petrified, her eyes staring in disbelief. Ralph hauled himself up beside her, putting his arm around her and holding her tight as they watched in horror.

The hideous idol was engulfed in smoke and flame that lit up the whole arena. As they watched the awesome spectacle an impossible thing started to happen, the idol began to move. First its head, then its limbs, eyes stared out from the beast's head, eyes as red as the hottest fire; eyes that pierced deep into one's soul.

Helen pulled herself away and scrambled into the darkness behind Ralph.

"Let's get away from here!" she cried. "It's evil, horribly evil."

Ralph did not move. He seemed petrified. His eyes were staring wildly at the beast. Helen pulled at him and tried to drag him away but she wasn't strong enough. Suddenly the beast lifted its ugly head and roared. It was a sound the like of which she had never heard before, so horrible, so blood-curdling that she let go of Ralph and clasped her hands over her ears as she fell to the ground. With the roar came a hot wind with a foul-smelling stench, shaking the trees and bushes around them.

Ralph seemed to come to at the terrible sound of the beast and he turned, looking for Helen.

"My God, did you see it! Did you see that thing?" he cried, his eyes still staring in terror.

Helen looked up at him, tears rolling down her cheeks.

"Please, Ralph," she cried, "Let's get away while we can."

"Not yet, not yet!" he giggled hysterically. "I must see more, I must see more!" and he turned away from her.

Just then there was a great shout from the arena. Helen jumped up to see what had happened. When she looked down a woman was standing in front of the idol, which had reverted to stone.

"It's her, it's Mary Bamford!" Ralph said, seemingly regaining some of his composure. "Just look at her, you wouldn't dream that she had so much power over people. Just look at them, how they adore her. She looks more like an angel than a Devil."

Helen looked at him and felt a little jealous at the way he was watching her. She stared in hatred at the woman and her strength rushed back into her body, making her more determined than ever to defeat her.

As Mary Bamford stood in full view of her disciples, she let her white flimsy robe drop from her milky white shoulders onto the marble steps and she stood naked before them.

A great cry went up from all around, it was the signal for debauchery unlimited. Sex-crazed men and women threw off their robes and began to seduce one another. Perversion was rife. There was shameless sex between men and men, women and women, and perverts of all kinds had their way with animals.

Helen turned away to be sick and staggered off into the woods. She had seen enough. Ralph turned to say something to her and seeing her moving away followed her.

"You're right," he said reassuringly, putting his arm around her.

But she pulled away from him shouting.

"You are no better than they are. Sitting there watching their filthy goings-on. You were enjoying it. Did it bring back memories, seeing her naked body?" and she held out her phial of holy water, shouting "Maybe you should have some of this to take the evil out of you!" and with this she threw the holy water into his face.

She never expected such a dramatic effect. Ralph flung his hands up, clutching wildly at his head and face and he ran screaming blindly through the trees.

"Oh, my God!" she cried out after him. "What have I done? Ralph, Ralph!" she called as she ran through the undergrowth with her skirt held high.

She hadn't gone very far when she stopped, realising that she had no hope of catching him.

The further she went away from the arena the quieter it was. She stopped now and then to see if she could hear anything but there wasn't any sign of Ralph anywhere.

It was about an hour later, after tramping the woods and looking around the outskirts of the old house, that she decided to make for the inn. As she approached the broken wall she heard a noise like someone moaning. She stood, still petrified at what it might be, her eyes staring wildly from side to side straining to see what was in the shadows.

The noise came again, but this time a name was called out very faint and very weak "Helen!"

She started forward into the shadows, searching amongst the undergrowth, rummaging through the bracken and the briars. Her hands were cut and bleeding as she came across a figure lying in a ditch beside the wall. She jumped down alongside the figure and held out her hand, gently touching its arm.

"Ralph, is that you?" she said softly.

"Helen!" came the reply from the crumpled figure of Ralph.

Ralph was lying on his left side, his face pressed into the bottom of the muddy ditch.

"Come on, my love," she said trying to get him up. "Let's have a good look at you."

Ralph seemed to realise that she was there and opened his eyes.

"I've been looking for you everywhere," he said in a faint voice. "We've got to get away from here. There's no time to lose!" and he tried to stand up but his strength had gone and he fell again into the mud.

"Everything's all right, my love, just take it easy for a while," she said, helping him to a sitting position.

"What happened to you? Why did you run away?"

"I don't know what's happened," he replied groggily. "My head! Something's happened to my head. I remember the flashing lights and the gunfire and I ran."

"You must have been back on the Somme, darling," she said trying to comfort him. "Come on, let's try and get you cleaned up a bit," she added, ripping her petticoat to make a cloth.

She tried the best she could but it wasn't easy down in a ditch in almost total darkness.

"That will have to do for the time being," she said, helping him to his feet. After struggling through the hole in the wall and the undergrowth on the other side they were soon on the road back to the inn. Ralph had completely recovered and was himself again, striding out boldly along the road with Helen having to run to keep up with him.

"I've been thinking," he said, suddenly stopping. "Which is the best thing to do? Should we go back to the inn or should we get in the car and drive to London tonight?"

Helen was taken aback at this suggestion. After all, her clothes were at the inn and she wanted to wash and clean up before she went anywhere. She told him as much.

They settled on going to the inn first and then home to London.

The inn was in darkness but luckily the front door was open, just as they had left it.

Upstairs in Helen's room they lit the solitary oil lamp that stood on the dressing table.

"There's only a jug and bowl to wash in," she said, pouring out the water. "I'll use it first because you're muddier than me!" she laughed, pointing at his face.

Ralph just smiled and sat on the bed to wait his turn. Sitting there he started to think of the night's events and as was his habit when thinking he stroked his face and chin. Suddenly he looked up in bewilderment and started to feel the left side of his face over and over again. Without warning he dashed to the bowl of water and pushed Helen aside as he splashed water all over his face. When he had finished he ran to the mirror on the dressing table and looked at his reflection.

"What's the matter with you?" Helen shouted angrily at him. "Can't you wait?"

Ralph took no notice of her. He was engrossed in his reflection. Suddenly he turned to her and holding the oil lamp up to his face he called out.

"Look at this! It's a miracle!"

"Look at what?" replied Helen, still annoyed with him.

"My face! My face!" he cried excitedly, coming over to her.

Helen looked up at him and her mouth dropped open at what she saw. She reached out and touched him on his cheek.

"Your scars, they've gone! Disappeared! But how? Oh, how wonderful!" she cried.

"It must have been the holy water," he cried, dancing around the room. "There's no other explanation for it, maybe it was twice as powerful with all that evil about."

"That must be it!" she called out to him as he danced around. "You looked that monster in the face, nobody else did, and when you turned and pushed me away your face was full of evil. The holy water not only cleansed the evil but removed the scars as well because they were evil-looking too."

He stopped dancing and looked at her. Touching his face he said "My God, I do believe you're right!"

CHAPTER TEN

After washing and a change of clothes they decided that they would leave the inn before dawn. They were too excited to sleep and went over the nights' events time and time again. Ralph had peeped into the cupboard to look at the picture but the frame was still empty.

"I was wondering about this place," he said. "Why doesn't it deteriorate like the rest of buildings she inhabits?"

"Maybe because it's being used every day," Helen replied.

"It must be something like that," he said, his eyes narrowing in deep thought. "This fellow Graylish must be some sort of custodian, he keeps this place running like an every day business. On the outside it's just an inn but in real life it's their meeting place, their headquarters."

"And her refuge, her sanctuary," butted in Helen.

"Yes, you're right!" enthused Ralph "This is her bolt hole, this place is safe for her at all times," and he sat on the edge of the bed.

"Why don't we destroy the place, set fire to it or something? That way she would have nowhere to hide, no permanent place to rest."

Helen looked aghast at him.

"We can't just set fire to it!" she said in horror at the suggestion. "We would end up in prison."

"But we've got to do something!" he retorted, getting angry. "This is the best chance we've had and we'll never get another like it. She is out of the place, over there in that bloody arena, the time to strike is now!" and he jumped up, opening the cupboard door. He stood for a moment looking at the empty picture frame, then suddenly he kicked at it, punching a great hole through the canvas.

Before he could pull his foot back, a scream shattered the still night air outside. Helen sprang from the bed and stood there, her eyes staring in terror at Ralph.

"What was that?" she cried "Oh my God, there's something out there!"

"I don't know" he replied, "But I think it's time we left."

Helen dashed to the door.

"Get to the car quickly!" he shouted after her. "I'll be right behind you."

As she ran off down the corridor Ralph grabbed the oil lamp and smashed it on the floor. The oil spread quickly across the polished wood, rapidly followed by eager flames reaching to burn everything in their path. Soon the whole room was ablaze. He stopped for a second to look at his handiwork and, satisfied he grabbed and threw every oil lamp he could find on his way to the front door.

Even as he reached the car, flames were licking up the insides of the windows.

"You did it!" she shouted at him. "You set fire to the place! Why?"

"To hell with the place and all in it!" he shouted back at her as the car burst into life and sped out onto the road.

"That's where they belong, in hell!"

They had only gone about five hundred yards when a group of people appeared in the glare of the headlights. They were all dressed in brown monks' habits.

Ralph was driving straight for them when Helen screamed: "It's them Ralph, it's them!" and she grabbed at the wheel, sending the car swerving from one side of the road to the other.

"What are you doing?" he shouted, pushing her away "Do you want to get us killed?"

"You were going straight for them!" she cried.

"So what!" he screamed at her in anger. "They deserve to die. You heard them, they are the Devil's spawn. It's either them or us. No quarter asked or given, just like the Somme."

The car picked up momentum as Ralph pressed hard on the accelerator. Trees, farmhouses and barns were there and gone in a flash as they sped along the narrow country lanes.

After about ten minutes' hard driving Helen shouted over the noise of the engine.

"Have you any idea where you are going? I'm sure we have passed that house before and I haven't noticed any direction signs."

Ralph slowed down and began to look ahead into the beam of the headlights. A barn appeared on the left hand side of the road and he stopped to have a closer look at it.

"I do believe you're right," he replied after a little deliberation. "Good God, we must have been going around in circles. All these blasted country roads look alike. I think there's a road to the left further up we'll take that and hope for the best."

The road turned out to be no more than a track with high hedgerows on either side. There were twists and turns every few yards.

"This can't be the right way," Helen called to him.

"Well there's nothing I can do for the moment," he shouted back. "I'll have to find a place to turn around before I can go back."

No sooner had he finished speaking he found that they were heading down a sharp incline and before he could stop the car they had plunged into a deep ford that ran across the track.

"Damn and blast it!" he shouted at the top of his voice as the water cascaded everywhere, but the engine was still running and he managed to drive slowly to the other side. He struggled with the engine for about another hundred yards or more but after many hiccups, splutters and bangs, combined with the sparks and a smell of burning, the car shook violently and stopped.

Ralph lent forward and placed his head between his hands on the steering-wheel.

"Damn! Damn! Damn!" he snorted between gritted teeth. "Damn and damn again!"

Helen looked out of the side window and started to giggle.

"I bet you feel a lot better for that!" she laughed. "Oh, hasn't it been a night to remember?" and she fell back on the seat in fits of laughter.

Ralph lifted up his head and looked at her as though she had gone mad but then he saw the funny side of it and joined in. Soon tears were streaming down their faces. Laughter had given them a relief from a nightmare.

It was twenty minutes or more before they had calmed down and Ralph put his arm around her, giving her a kiss. She in turn kissed him on the soft skin of his new-found features.

"This has been the most wonderful and yet the most horrific night in my whole life," she said softly, caressing his cheek.

"Yes, here we are," he said with a twinkle in his eye, "Yes, here we are wrapped in each other's arms, a beautiful moon above, freezing cold, wet through and sitting in a clapped-out car in the middle of nowhere."

"You swine, Ralph Grant!" she shouted at him as she threw a punch and missed for by this time he had jumped out of the car laughing.

"I'm going down the road to find civilisation," he called to her from in front of the car.

"Ralph! Ralph!" she screamed "Don't leave me!" as she scrambled out of the car and ran after him down the track.

It was three in the morning and they had walked a good two miles without seeing a sign of human habitation. Ralph stopped suddenly and looked across the open field to a wood on their right.

"There's something over there," he said, pointing towards the moon over the wood. "There must be a house in the woods, can you see the smoke drifting up across the face of the moon?

"Come on, we'll investigate" he said, climbing over a small stone wall and helping her to follow him.

The wood was further than they had thought and by the time they had reached it Helen was out of breath.

"I'll have to rest for a while," she said, leaning against a tree.

Ralph walked on a few yards into the wood and peered through the trees into the darkness.

"There's something there further back in the woods," he said quietly. "Now we'll have to be careful and on our guard at all times. We don't know what this place is or who it belongs to, there may be dogs and God knows what else. After tonight's experiences we can expect anything."

Helen didn't like the sound of that and quickly placed her crucifix on the outside of her top coat. Ralph smiled as he watched her firmly pat the cross, as though to say: "Right, I'm ready for anything."

"Good girl," he said giving her a kiss. "Now then, are you ready?"

Helen nodded in the affirmative and holding hands Ralph led the way. It wasn't long before they had reached the edge of the wood and were looking across a clearing at the dark shape of a building. Ralph stopped, cautious of any further approach. He crouched down behind a tree pulling Helen with him.

"What's the matter?" she whispered.

"I don't know," he replied, quietly. "It's just a feeling" and he stared long and hard at the black shape before them.

"I don't know what it is," he carried on, "But somehow or other this place seems familiar, as though I've been here before."

"How can you say that?" she whispered. "It's dark, places look alike in the dark."

He didn't reply. The gut feeling was still there. It was just as though he was waiting to go 'over the top' during the war, a feeling that he would never forget.

"You stay here," he turned and said to her in a commanding voice, "and I mean here, do you understand? Don't move a muscle. I won't be long, I'm just going to have a quick scout around. I'll be back in a minute," and with this he was gone from her sight.

Helen crouched low down into the roots of the tree, pressing herself up against the bark and trying her best to mingle with Mother Nature. She was scared stiff at the slightest sound and her every nerve was on a knife's edge. Suddenly there was a rustling sound close by her and she nearly let out a scream.

"Where are you?" came Ralph's whispering voice from behind her.

She moved to a sitting position.

"Here!" she replied, trying to keep her voice down.

Ralph came up and grabbed her by the arm then he pulled away into the trees until they were a safe distance from the house. When he stopped she said "What's wrong? What did you find out?"

"You won't believe it," he said quietly. "It's crazy."

"What is?" she said, getting annoyed with him.

"Well," he started, "You remember the cottage up in the Lake District? The one that was derelict, the one that Sittwell ran from?"

"Yes, yes!" she replied with even more impatience.

"This cottage is an exact replica, if not, then it's the same one," he said, fully expecting her to scoff at the suggestion but no ridicule came from her. Instead she just looked at him and thought for a while.

"How can you be so sure?" she eventually asked.

"I know that place inside out," he replied. "Don't that forget I spent one hell of a week in that place. Do you think I'd forget that?"

"Yes, I know, my love," she said tenderly. "But what's the significance of it? What does it all mean?"

"I've been thinking about that," he said softly. "This must be her sanctuary, not the inn. She can create this anywhere but what baffles me is why not the Manor? She was high born, she was a lady, it doesn't make any sense."

They were quiet for a moment then the early morning call of a cockerel from a distant farm brought them sharply back to reality.

"I think we had better get moving," he said, walking away from the cottage. "It will soon be light and maybe we can get the car fixed somewhere in this godforsaken hole."

They were in luck. A passing farmer with great Shire horse gave them a tow to the nearest garage and as luck had it again the mechanic was an ex-army transport man with a great deal of knowledge on staff cars.

"Ex-Sgt Robinson, that's me, sir," he said, giving Ralph a salute.

"I knows an officer when I sees one," he said, shifting his huge frame towards the car. "Used to be a blacksmith before the war but they taught me to mend these instead. Now sir, what seems to be the trouble?"

He was a giant of a man, six feet four of bone and muscle. Black curly hair covered his head and strong blue eyes sparkled with merriment as he spoke. It was five thirty in the morning but there he was, with his shirt sleeves rolled up, talkative, happy and ready to help.

"You look as if you've been up all night, miss," he laughed.

"Now why don't you go and see my Betty, she'll see to you while I get on with this," he said lifting the car bonnet.

Helen's tired eyes lit up when she heard this and she wandered off in the direction of the little house that stood behind the garage.

"Have you lived around these parts long?" asked Ralph.

"All my life so far," laughed the big man with his head stuck under the bonnet.

"Is there a large house in these parts known as Bamford Hall or Manor?" Ralph asked casually.

"Bamford Manor? Why that's just down the road about four miles," the big man said "If you're going there you can't miss it, it's the biggest house in these parts. Stands on the right of the road."

"I heard that it was derelict and overgrown," said Ralph searching for information.

"Why, God bless you, no sir!" the big man laughed. "It was taken over by the brass hats, beggin' your pardon, sir, during the war and Lady Bamford still lives there."

"Wasn't there some talk of witchcraft in the family?" Ralph pressed on.

“My word you’re going back a bit sir,” the mechanic said, diving once again under the bonnet brandishing a spanner.

“Yes, that would be Lady Mary that would, bit of a rum one you might say. The story goes that she has a cottage in the woods and she lures young men there and then has her way with them.”

He roared with laughter: “I could do with a bit of that myself now and again.”

“It’s strange that she should use a cottage,” laughed Ralph with him. “You know, when she’s got that plush mansion and all those rooms she could run around in.”

They both rolled about laughing.

“She could chase me any time!” roared the big man. Then when he had calmed down a bit he said: “They do say as she is frightened to use the Manor because she was burnt to death in a great house up North, something to do with Cromwell’s men, I think,” and he disappeared again under the bonnet.

“They do say,” he said popping up again with oil on his face, “They do say that if she is caught in the Manor t’would be the end of her. That is to say if it was on fire like the first one. They reckons that they can’t go through it twice, but it’s all old wives’ tales. What do you think, sir?”

“I suppose you’re right,” replied Ralph trying to contain his excitement.

“Oh, talking about fires, sir,” said the big man. “There was a big fire at the Raven Inn that’s not far from here. They say it was burnt to the ground, they do.”

“Oh, when was that?” asked Ralph looking uninterested.

“Why only last night, sir,” he replied. “Right mess it was. They thinks that the landlord had something to do with it because he hasn’t been seen since. Mind you, nobody ever used the place, so I don’t suppose it matters much.”

He stood up, stretching himself.

“Now, sir, would you care to start her up?”

After a few minor adjustments the car was running sweetly and an invitation to breakfast couldn’t be refused after a good wash and brush down. Two hours later they were on their way again heading for Bamford Manor.

“I’ve been longing to tell you,” Ralph said excitedly, “but I couldn’t bring up the subject again in front our friend the ex-blacksmith, he might have thought that I was obsessed with witchcraft.”

“Ha!” snorted Helen. “That’s a laugh…”’

"Well, I was right all along," he carried on, ignoring her remarks.

"It seems that the local legend regarding the Lady Mary has presented us with a plan of action and maybe, and I say that with some reservation, maybe a final solution to the whole messy situation."

"What are you talking about?" Helen said, turning to him and following her remarks with a loud yawn. "Oh, I could sleep for a week," and she closed her eyes and curled up on the seat.

"Huh!" Ralph said as he looked at her.

"Here's me with exciting news!" he thought, "and she goes to sleep. Well, I can't blame her, it was a rough night. It might be a good idea to pull in to some quiet spot and have forty winks."

Taking a side road to the left he drove up a steep hill. On top of the hill was a small wood and he parked the car in amongst the trees.

"This will do nicely," he said and he settled down to a well-deserved rest. He slept peacefully enough but something in his subconscious was telling him to wake. He denied the feeling for as long as he could but in the end the feeling was too strong for him and he opened his eyes.

The car windows were covered in condensation or that was what he first thought, but as he tried to wipe them with a cloth he realised that it wasn't condensation at all but a dense fog that had descended on the hill.

He looked down at Helen sleeping peacefully and smiled, but as he turned and stretched his heart leapt within him, for there standing in front of the car was a figure, a tall dark figure of a man dressed in Puritan clothes.

Ralph's heart was pounding for he immediately recognised the figure and the form to be none other than Father Ross. The figure beckoned him.

He looked down at Helen and then again at Father Ross. Thinking that Helen would be safe enough, he slowly opened the door and stood facing his old friend.

The face of the priest showed no expression: it was white and drawn. He turned and walked a few paces, beckoning to Ralph to follow him. Ralph was reluctant and turned to the car holding out his hand. The priest stopped, came over and looked into the car where he saw Helen asleep. Then he did a strange thing, he took off his crucifix, his beloved gold crucifix, and he kissed it before he hung it on the door handle beside Helen. This done he once again walked off into the fog, beckoning Ralph to follow.

Ralph's mind was in a turmoil.

"What was he doing here? Where was he taking him? Why should he suddenly turn up like this and especially now, so soon after last night's traumatic experience?"

The black form of the priest pressed on through the fog with Ralph following a good five yards back. Suddenly he stopped and pointed out into the dense fog. Ralph looked in the same direction but couldn't see a thing. Thc fog began to disperse, then disappear altogether. He found himself looking down on the Manor House in all its glory. No longer was it derelict but a fine new-looking building. People were in the gardens, horsemen were riding through the gate, flags were raised high on the turrets. They were back in the seventeenth century.

Ralph looked in wonderment at the old priest. Father Ross stood for a moment surveying the scene then he bowed his head and crossed himself. Turning once more he pointed to a rock at the edge of the wood then back to the Manor. He did this several times.

"He's telling me something" thought Ralph. "Something to do with that rock and the house."

Ralph pointed at the rock and the priest waved his arm towards it.

"He wants me to go to it," he said aloud and off he set, scrambling down a slippery slope. He reached the rock and started to look around but he couldn't see anything of importance. Then suddenly he noticed a clump of bushes. On further investigation he found a hole running beneath the rock directly behind the bushes. It was big enough for a man to pass through. Ralph lay flat on the ground and pushed his head and shoulders into the hole.

"It's a tunnel!" he cried, excitedly. "A bolt-hole! An escape passage from the Manor, and if one can get out, I can get in any time I like."

He climbed back up the slope to where the old priest was standing. Before he had reached the top the fog was all about them.

Once again Father Ross led the way, with Ralph following close behind.

It wasn't long before the priest stopped and pointed ahead of him. Ralph came up beside him for the first time and they stood looking at each other. Then came the first sign of expression on the old man's face as he saw Ralph's newly-formed skin. He reached out, touching it, and as he did so a tear trickled down his cheek.

Ralph smiled and went to touch him, but as he reached out the priest disappeared.

CHAPTER ELEVEN

With the closing of the car door Helen woke with a start.

"What is it? What's wrong?" she cried out.

"It's amazing what people can miss when they fall asleep!" laughed Ralph.

"What do you mean?" she asked, sitting up and looking bewildered. "What's happened?"

"While you were having your beauty sleep," he said smugly, "I had a visitation."

Helen's eyes opened wide in horror.

"Not her, it wasn't her, was it?" she cried, grabbing hold of his arm.

"No, it wasn't her," he laughed, trying to calm her down. "But it was someone from the past, an old friend of mine."

"Father Ross?" she cried. "Father Ross was here? Oh, Ralph, why didn't you wake me?" Then she looked at him with narrowing eyes and said "You're not having me on are you? You didn't dream this up just for fun did you? Because if you did, Ralph Grant…"

All the time she was going on, Ralph was holding the old priest's gold crucifix in his hand and before she could finish he showed it to her.

A gasp of amazement left her, as she stared in wonderment at the ancient cross and she took it in both hands as though it was a delicate flower.

"Oh, Ralph," she whispered in awe as she fondled it. "It's true he was here. Oh, I wish I could have seen him, it must have been a wonderful experience."

"I'll tell you all about it as we go along," he said starting up the car.

"We have a lot to do and plans to make. The old priest showed me the way and now it's up to us," and he told her all that had happened while she was sleeping.

The town of Aylesbury provided them with an ideal base, a good hotel to rest up in and plan their next move, and plenty of shops to gather all the requirements that they would need in their assault on the evil that lurked within the walls of Bamford Manor.

On the third night they were ready. The car was loaded with three oil lamps, two gallons of paraffin, one gallon of holy water (which raised a few eyebrows in the local parish church), a garden spray, Father Ross's book and the golden crucifix. Ralph checked everything thoroughly.

"We can't leave anything to chance," he said as they set off. "It's now or never. We'll only get one bite at this apple and if we miss, God knows what will happen to us."

Helen did not reply. To think of what might happen was too much for her. She had seen enough on the first occasion and she had resigned herself to the fact that what must be must be.

Few words were said as they sped onwards through the blackness of the night. Rain started to splatter on the windscreen and before long they were in the middle of a thunderstorm. Lightning flashed all around and great claps of thunder rent the air. The wind was at gale strength and shook the car like a toy.

Ralph slowed the car down to a crawl. He knew that they were somewhere near to the blacksmith's garage.

"There's a track up on the left," he called out to Helen. "Keep an eye open for it."

Helen nodded and wiped the window with her scarf. The rain was still lashing down and a few moments later she called out.

"There, I think we have just passed it."

Ralph stopped the car then began to back it slowly according to her directions.

"Stop!" she called. "Is this the turning?"

"We'll soon find out," he said, driving the car along the track.

His sense of direction had not left him. Even though it was pitch black and pouring with rain he could pinpoint an area within a few square yards, just as he had done in the war as a field officer.

Pulling up amongst the trees on top of the hill they sat in silence for a few minutes, listening to the rain bouncing off the roof of the car. It was Helen who first broke the uneasy quiet.

"Ralph," she said, taking his hand. "No matter what happens tonight I want you to know that I love you and I trust you to make all the right decisions. If anything should go wrong I won't blame you because we are in this together."

He leaned over and kissed her.

"There's just one more thing," she carried on, "I'm scared to death."

"Well, just for the record," he replied, "so am I!"

They held each other for a little while and then he said.

"Well, are we ready?"

They left the car with what they hoped would be their weapons of destruction. Apprehension on Helen's part was fast becoming stark terror, as the howling wind and lashing rain turned each tree that surrounded them into a creaking squealing monster, with a hundred arms that reached out for her.

Reaching the spot where Father Ross had stood, Ralph pointed down the slope.

"It's down there, somewhere," he called over the noise of the storm. "Be careful, it's treacherous," and he led the way down, doing his best to help Helen as they descended the mud-sodden bank. After a slip or two and one near-disaster when they nearly lost the holy water and all the paraffin they eventually arrived at the bottom.

The gale force wind was even stronger, so strong that they could hardly stand against it and the torrential rain was icy, stinging their faces as it lashed into them. They struggled on through muddy water that was running off the bank in streams until after about fifty yards the rock loomed up in front of them.

"Here it is!" he shouted to her. "Try to find somewhere for shelter. I'll look for the opening," and he left her leaning up against a niche in the rock face.

It wasn't long before he was back again.

"I've found it!" he called. "But it will be difficult to get to it , there are thorn bushes blocking the entrance."

As the lightning flashed and the thunder roared all around, they stood looking at the dense thorn bushes.

"We'll never get through there!" she shouted over the noise.

"You look after these," he called, putting his load beside her. "I'll see what I can do," and he went forward, reaching out towards the bushes.

Suddenly the wind swirled round and round. making a terrible howling noise. The thorn bushes seem to rise up and a thousand barbed whips lashed out at him in defence of their secret. Staggering back, cut and bleeding, he swore.

"Jesus, they're alive!"

"Burn them!" Helen shouted, furious at what she had seen, and without thinking she opened a can of paraffin and threw it on top of the bushes.

"No!" he screamed but it was too late and he stood, arms raised, as he watched the precious oil drain away.

"Well," he said, turning to her, "We'll have to try it now."

He reached down into his trouser pocket and produced a box of matches. Taking a piece of note paper from his pocket, he soaked it in paraffin from the remaining bottle. Then picking up a stone from nearby he wrapped thc paper around it. He stood as close to the bushes as he dared and bending over he opened his top coat to shield the striking match from the wind. He had to be quick, for no sooner had the flame touched the paper than it flared up in his hand. Standing up he tossed the flaming ball into the oil soaked bushes.

For a few seconds his heart stood still. The flaming ball flickered as though it was about to die, but then there was a great flash as the bushes burst into flame, sending him reeling back from the blast and heat. The howling wind did the rest. Soon there was very little left of the thorny whips that had barred their way.

Hacking away at what was left he soon found the entrance to the priest's bolt-hole.

"I don't know what it will be like down there," he called to her. "I'll go first and light a lamp. When I'm through, pass me the rest of the stuff."

"Anything's better than being out here!" she called back to him. "Please hurry."

He went through feet first on his stomach feeling around for solid ground to stand on. Suddenly it was there, no more than five feet below.

Making sure of his position he called to her to pass the lamps and the oil. As the light flickered forth Ralph looked around, a few feet away rough-hewn steps descended into the darkness.

"Here I come!" came Helen's voice from the hole.

After helping her down and lighting another lamp he filled the garden spray with holy water.

"I don't know if it will work," he said, feeling his way down the steps, "But it's the best thing I could think of," and he pushed it down the front of his coat.

"Keep about six feet behind me," he called to her. "Just in case, you never know what's going to happen."

There were twenty steps in all. Ralph counted them slowly as they descended.

"So far, so good," he said, as they looked into darkness that lay ahead.

"Do you think it's safe?" Helen asked as Ralph moved slowly forward. "It won't cave in or anything will it?"

"God knows," he replied. "But we'll have to be as quiet as possible. I suppose the slightest sound could do anything, after all it's a hell of a long time since anyone used this passage."

Part of the tunnel was solid rock and part was man-made. It was narrow, sometimes only eighteen inches wide, but always going down. Water was seeping in through the man-made parts and sometimes they had to wade through deep puddles. They had been going for about an hour and a half when the tunnel came to an abrupt end.

"Oh Hell!" Ralph said, holding up the light. "Now what do we do?"

"There must have been collapse at some time," Helen said, coming forward. Ralph held the light nearer to the dead-end wall and touched it.

"There's been no fall here," he said, giving the wall a closer inspection. "It's smooth," and he banged it with his fist saying: "This is solid rock."

As his fist struck the wall, dust dropped down and a crack appeared. He held the light closer.

"Helen, there's a door here. Please hold my lamp while I give it a push."

Helen took the lamp and Ralph pushed at the door with all his strength. Suddenly it moved, only an inch, but it moved.

"It's on a swivel," he said. "See, if I push this side the other side comes out. I'll put my back on this side and my feet against the wall opposite, in that way I'll get better leverage."

"Be careful, don't hurt yourself!" Helen said, a little nervous at what might happen.

Ralph got himself into position and gave a mighty heave. Without warning the door gave way. Helen gave an almighty scream as the part of the door swung into the tunnel, catapulting out a skeleton dressed in seventeenth century clothes. As it hit the floor, dust flew everywhere, the clothes disintegrated and the head of the skeleton rolled off down the tunnel.

"Oh my God!" she cried hysterically, staring at the skull. Then she turned to look for Ralph who had disappeared into the opening in a cloud of dust.

"Ralph!" she cried, "Ralph where are you?"

As the dust settled she saw him lying prostrate in the midst of more skeletons. She screamed again: "Ralph! Ralph!"

"I'm all right," he said calmly. "Get a grip of yourself, they can't hurt you. I would have thought that you would have been used to seeing things like this by now, after what you went through in the War."

"That was different," she cried "This is horrible."

There were six skeletons in all.

"They must have been Catholic priests hiding from the Protestants," he said. "See there are crucifixes everywhere."

"I don't care what they were," she cried. "It's horrible, they must have starved to death trapped behind this wall."

"Pass me a light, love," he said, holding out his hand. "This must lead somewhere."

"Oh, I wish we had never come!" she said, shivering with fright and trying not to look at the unfortunate priests.

"Are you going to pass that oil lamp to me or not?" he said, getting a little cross. "The amount of noise we have made is enough to waken the dead and we have certainly disturbed these chaps."

"Do you think anyone heard?" she said, passing the lamp at long last.

"Can't be sure," he replied, lifting the lamp and looking around. "We won't know until we get up there, that's if we ever get up there."

Then he went quiet as though he was studying something.

"This must be it," he said at long last. "Come here a moment and hold the lamp for me."

Helen didn't like the sound of that. It meant that she had to go and stand amongst the skeletons but she plucked up enough courage to do as he asked. She found him standing on a stone that jutted out from the wall about three feet from the floor. He was pressing up against part of the ceiling. The room was very tiny, no more than six feet by three, but it was quite high. She took the lamp from him and watched as he pushed.

Soon there was a little movement and it wasn't long before they could feel fresh air blowing into the little room. But whatever room was above them was in complete darkness. Ralph pushed the flagstone to one side.

"Pass the lamp," he whispered.

As the light shone into the inky blackness above he could see that they had emerged into some sort of kitchen or large storeroom. Ralph put the lamp on the floor and pulled himself up.

"Pass the bottles and the lamp up," he whispered, "then I'll pull you up."

When this was done they stood looking around at their strange surroundings.

"This place hasn't been used for ages," Helen said quietly. "I wonder what it was?"

"Some kind of meat kitchen or slaughter-house," he replied. "Look at the huge hooks in the ceiling and this stone table in the middle."

"Oh, the thought of that makes me shudder," she said, rubbing her arms. Ralph picked up a lamp and moved towards the door. Helen followed.

"Now not a word," he whispered, "No matter what you see or hear, silence is imperative, you've got to be brave, all right, my love?"

Her beautiful green eyes were wide with frightened expectation, and she swallowed hard before nodding her head in reply.

Ralph reached for the door handle and gave it a twist followed by a sharp tug. The door gave a groan and a squeak as it opened a few inches. Ralph took a peep outside, then opening the door wide he motioned for her to follow.

They had entered a very large room: it was the main kitchen. There were two large tables in the centre but like the other room it was bare. A stone staircase led up to the floor above and Ralph, lamp held high, started to climb it with Helen in close attendance.

The door at the top of the stairs opened easily and they stood looking down a long wide hall-way with doors on either side. This too was void of furniture or trappings of any description. Great cobwebs hung from the ceiling and dust covered everything. They had only taken a few paces down the hall when a slight breeze gently rocked the cobwebs to and fro. They stopped and looked at each other, the lamps flickering as they held them. Then Helen suddenly gripped Ralph's arm and stared at him in horror as ghostly music and laughter drifted along with the breeze.

"Oh, my God," she whispered in terror.

Ralph lifted his hand up for silence and they stood there listening to the eerie sounds.

"Let's go back," she said, tugging at his arm. "I'm frightened "

"Can't go back now," he whispered. "There's too much at stake, we must see it through to the end.

He carried on slowly down the hall with Helen hanging on to him. They were half way along the hall when a strange thing happened. The once-dusty floor suddenly became highly polished and everywhere little bursts of light were dancing and bouncing from the ceiling onto the walls, then to the floor and up again. There seemed to be thousands of them.

Ralph and Helen crouched down in a wide doorway, Helen hiding her face behind the door and Ralph shielding his eyes with his hand at the bright spectacle.

"What's happening?" she cried with her face pressed hard against the door jamb.

No sooner had it started than the whole thing stopped. Ralph stood in shocked silence. The place was transformed the cobwebs and dust were all gone. The hall was a showpiece of elegance: chairs covered in tapestry, and large inlaid sideboards that were weighed down with silver trays, cups and goblets. Huge oil paintings covered the walls and the whole was capped by a majestic oak panelled ceiling, but there was a smell, a sweet nauseating smell, that accompanied the change. It took him only a few seconds to realise that the smell was the sickly smell of death and that the Lady of the Manor was back in residence.

He felt a tug on his sleeve and it shocked him back to reality.

"How can this happen?" Helen whispered, looking about her bewildered at the transformation.

"Witchcraft, magic, devilry, call it what you like!" he replied, cautiously looking up and down the hall.

"We saw enough thc other night to realise that we can expect anything. This is her personal trademark, it happens everywhere she goes. This just tells us to beware, we have been warned of her arrival."

Ralph tried some of the doors that led off the hall but they were all locked. Suddenly a snarling noise came from behind. Ralph and Helen looked around in terror. Walking slowly towards them were three large black Mastiffs, their eyes glowing red and their pendulous lips curling back showing their huge fangs. Foam dripped from their strong jaws as they made ready to pounce.

"Run!" shouted Ralph, as he threw his oil lamp at the dogs. The lamp smashed a few feet in front of them. Flames shot across the floor but it didn't stop them. Onward they came snarling, barking, growling. Ralph snatched the brass spray from under his coat to use as a weapon. In his panic to defend himself he completely forgot about the holy water contained in it. He swung wildly as the Mastiffs sprang at him, one tore at his sleeve, another his trouser leg. He kicked out, sending one of them sliding across the floor, but back it came even more furious than before.

He was now backing up to where Helen was screaming at the end of the hall. She was tugging for all she was worth at a door handle. As he swung once more with the spray a small amount of holy water squirted out and splashed into the face of one of the dogs. It stood up on its hind legs its ugly head not more than a foot away from his. He could feel its hot foul smelling breath. Then the snarls of the beast suddenly turned into howls of terror as its face began to burn. Flesh curled back from its skull and it dropped on the floor at his feet. The beast howled and clawed at its skinless head as it writhed in agony around the floor. Then suddenly it was dead.

Strangely enough the other two beasts stood back and watched the third member of their pack die. But in those few precious moments Ralph realised the power in the spray and he attacked, pushing the pump for all he was worth. As the holy water was discharged into the air it fell in a wide arc over the attacking beasts. As before the animals' skin started to burn and they were so incensed with the terrible pain that they attacked each other. It wasn't very long before they all lay dead. Ralph stood there ashen and shaking from head to toe, looking at the smouldering carcasses.

He was just about to walk to where Helen was standing by the door when he noticed something strange and went over to have a closer look.

"Come and look at this!" he spoke in whispered tones to Helen.

She came towards him very slowly, still not sure of the dogs even though they were dead.

"That was horrible!" she said, concerned for his welfare. "Are you all right?"

"Oh yes, I'm all right," he replied, not sounding too affected by what had happened but more excited by what he had found.

"Look at this," he said, pointing at the floor. "The dust has returned where the holy water fell. Do you see what this means, we can make all this disappear."

"But we haven't enough for that!" Helen replied, still keeping her distance from the dogs.

"I know that," he answered in a huff, as he refilled the spray from the gallon bottle. "But it's a marvellous weapon, we can use it against anything that stands in our way. Good old Father Ross, he was right all the time. How did his poem go 'Gird thyself with cross and water...' Well, we have his cross and plenty of holy water."

"Another thing," he said excitedly, "This proves that all this is an illusion, we only think we see it."

"Those dogs are no illusion," she said shuddering, "and the tears in your coat and trousers are no illusion either."

"Hmm," he muttered, looking at the large rip in his sleeve and then at the dead Mastiffs. "I suppose you're right, but it did save us, didn't it?"

"There's no denying that," she replied. "But these were dogs, what about her and that horrible thing in the amphitheatre the other night? Will it stop them?"

"I believe it will," he replied with determination. "I believe in God and the tools that Father Ross has given me to destroy this evil woman. I am the only one to escape from her clutches and I owe a debt to Father Ross and all the people of the valley for making it so. I am their instrument and the means towards their everlasting peace and salvation. This woman shall not prevail. The evil witch shall be destroyed and sent into everlasting damnation."

Helen stood open-mouthed at this outburst. This wasn't her Ralph talking, it was a completely different person speaking through him. It wasn't even his voice. He had suddenly turned into a seventeenth century witch-finder.

"Ralph! Ralph!" she cried tugging at his torn sleeve. "Ralph, what's the matter with you?"

He did not answer her beseeching plea but turned away shouting "The Lord of Hosts will seek her out and I shall be there to reap his retribution" and marched off towards the door at the end of the hall.

"Ralph!" she screamed after him "Ralph, stop, please stop!"

But her cries fell on deaf ears. He was possessed by an existence from another life, a life not of her time. An existence from the dark pages of history when witches were a reality, something to be feared and hated.

She found him standing on the grand marble staircase with Father Ross's gold crucifix held high above his head, shouting, "Come out, daughter of Satan, sister of Endor and face the Lord God of Hosts!"

He took a few steps towards the top, his voice echoing around the huge edifice. Standing on the landing overlooking the grand hall he yelled out, quoting from Psalm 21:

"Your hand will lay hold on all your enemies
our right hand will seize your foes.
At the time of your appearing you will make
Them like a fiery furnace.
In his wrath the Lord will swallow them up
And his fire will consume them.
You will destroy their descendants from the earth
Their posterity from Mankind.
Though they plot evil against you and devise
Wicked schemes they cannot succeed."

Helen stood at the foot of the staircase frightened out of her wits.

"Ralph! Ralph!" she screamed at the top of her voice.

Suddenly the Manor reverted back to its original state and a cold biting wind swept down the staircase, whipping up the dust into clouds. The ground began to tremble and pieces of plaster started to fall from the ornamental ceiling, crashing onto the marble floor.

"Ralph, for God's sake, Ralph!" Helen screamed at him. "Come down! Come down or you'll be killed!"

He didn't take any notice of her. He just stood there shouting from the scriptures:

"Yea, though I walk through the Valley

Of the Shadow of Death,

I will fear no evil."

At the word 'evil' the wind howled in defiance. Ralph's white hair was standing on end, his top coat blowing straight out behind him. He looked mad and defiant of all about him. The large oak doors at the entrance had been ripped off by the howling wind and blown out into the night. Helen was hanging on for her life to a marble pillar close to the gaping hole that the doors had left.

"Ralph!" she tried to scream out, but the raging wind took her breath away.

Everything was shaking and moving. Great gaps appeared in the floor as the marble began to disappear into the cellar below. The grand staircase collapsed in a tremendous roar, walls began to totter and fall. Suddenly the howling wind turned into a cyclone that shot up towards Ralph and lifted him high as it tore a gigantic hole in the roof and carried him with it into the blackness of the night.

Helen, who had witnessed the whole terrifying incident, threw her arms up in horror towards him, releasing her grip on the pillar, and was blown towards the trees in front of the crumbling house. For a few moments she lay there trying to contemplate what had happened. Then she sat up and watched as the old Manor crashed moaning, creaking, screeching like an animal in its dying throes. She moved back into the trees crying.

"I knew it would end this way," she sobbed. "Why wouldn't he listen to me? Oh God, if there is a God up there," she shouted at the sky through the trees, "what have you done to him?"

As she staggered hurt and bewildered through the wood, a dog could be heard baying at the moon.

CHAPTER TWELVE

The whole countryside was shaken by what the locals thought was an earthquake. At dawn the police, who consisted of a sergeant and two constables, enlisted the aid of scores of the local inhabitants to search through the debris of the old Manor. Never had such a thing happened before and they were concerned about the whereabouts of Lady Bamford. It wasn't until late morning that they found Helen asleep in the car. She was covered in dust and dirt. She had several cuts about her face and when they woke her she was rambling about dogs, scriptures, and a man named Ralph who had gone through the roof, blown there by a cyclone. They sent for an ambulance to take her to the local cottage hospital.

It was a week before Helen was feeling anything like her old self and it was the same period of time before the doctor would allow the police to ask her any questions about that fateful night. She had gone to hell and back in those few days. Her mind had been tormented by hideous macabre spectres, monsters, half-man half-beast, black Mastiffs with blood spurting out of their eyes, and Mary Bamford carrying her beloved Ralph down to hell as he screamed out for her to save him.

It was on a Sunday afternoon that Dr Bishop came into her tiny room. He was a small quietly-spoken man, gentle in every respect, and her confidence in him grew with every visit. He was about fifty years of age and his hair, although going grey, was wiry and unruly. His eyes were a sparkling blue which seemed to give her a sense of friendship and trust.

"Now, young lady," he said sitting on the edge of the bed. "How are you feeling today?"

"I'm feeling fine, thank you, doctor," she replied with a smile.

"Are you well enough to receive a visitor?" he asked, taking her pulse.

"A visitor?" she asked, sitting up straight. "But who knows that I'm here?"

"It's surprising how word gets out in this day and age!" he answered, with a twinkle in his eyes.

"It's not…?" she started to say, but was interrupted by the doctor.

"Yes, who? Who were you going to say?" he said looking at her more intently.

"Oh, no-one," she replied, a bit sheepish.

"The reason I ask, young lady," he said, looking her directly in the eyes, "is because you have told me nothing of yourself except your name since you arrived here. Now I find out from a friend of yours from London that you are a nurse, not only a nurse, but a nurse with commendations won during the war in France. You are getting to be more of a surprise to me every day."

She bowed her head in shame, for she had indeed told him nothing. It wasn't that she didn't want to tell him, she did. But she couldn't take the chance that he might not believe her story. So she had kept quiet about that terrible night at the Manor.

The doctor could see that he wasn't going to get any more out of her and he stood up, saying "Right, miss, are you ready for your visitor?"

Helen nodded, her head still bent and her eyes still staring at the bedclothes in shame.

As the doctor left the room she wondered who the visitor might be.

"It can't be Ralph," she thought as tears filled her eyes. "Ralph has gone forever," and she was about to burst into tears when a voice said.

"So it is you, Miss Graham?"

Helen looked up in astonishment to see Inspector Sharp standing there.

At last here was someone she could tell everything to, someone who understood, and she cried out with joy, holding out her arms towards him as tears streamed down her face.

Inspector Sharp, big and cumbersome as he was, dashed to hold her in his comforting arms.

"Now, now, Miss what's all this for?" he said, stroking her hair. "You tell me what's been happening. I read all about the so-called earthquake in the London papers but I didn't take much notice of it until I saw the name Bamford. Then I got in touch with the local lads, they told me about you and here I am."

It took Helen a little while to regain her composure but when she did she told the Inspector all that had happened. He sat there open-mouthed at the terrible things she told him and after she had finished he stood up and paced about the small room, thinking.

"It's unbelievable! Incredible!" he said after a while. "No-one will believe us, you know. You understand that, don't you?"

"I've been thinking about that," she answered, looking up at him. "You see, Inspector there are things in my story, certain parts of it, that can be proven. For instance," she carried on, "ask the local police if they found any effects in the rubble of the old manor. You know, furniture, pictures, ornaments, that sort of thing. Also ask them if they found any remains of any kind."

"What kind of remains?" he asked, sitting on the bed.

"The only remains that can be there are those of the dogs," she replied. "We are the only people to know that and, if as they say around these parts that the Manor was lived in, where is the furniture, the pictures, the silver and so on? It can't all just disappear can it, or can it?"

"Point taken!" he said, smiling at her. "You'll make a good detective, Miss Graham, when all this is over I'll see about giving you a job at the Yard!"

"Please call me 'Helen', Inspector," she said, touching his hand. "You'll never know what you've done for me today and I would like to think that we are friends."

The big man looked shy for the first time and blushed as he said "That would suit me fine, miss, I mean 'Helen', and I'll sort this out if it's the last thing I do."

"Thank you," she answered. "I feel a hundred per cent better for your visit and I'll be out of here in no time at all."

"There's no rush for that," he said, going to the door. "I'm staying locally for a while. I've some leave due to me and I might as well take it now. You just look after yourself. I'll be in touch," and with that he left.

Two days later Helen was ready to leave the hospital but rather than go back to London she booked in at the George Hotel in Aylesbury.

She wanted to be near at hand if anything should happen. Ralph was still uppermost in her thoughts and she couldn't bring herself to believe that he was dead.

It was at the George Hotel that Inspector Sharp came to see her. Sitting in the lounge bar at a quiet corner table so that they couldn't be overheard, he related the latest events.

"You were right all the way through, young lady," he said in low tones. "There wasn't a stick of furniture to be found, no effects, nothing. And you were right on the second count as well. The carcasses of three dogs were found, all Mastiffs and all had died in very strange ways. The vet says that he's seen nothing like it and he's been practising for thirty years. Nobody can understand where Lady Bamford has disappeared to. They have contacted all her friends and some of those people look a little odd to say the least. They are linking it with the fire at the Raven Inn that happened a short while ago. The manager, a Mr Graylish, has also disappeared. But the strangest thing happened only an hour ago. I was at the local police station when I received a telephone call from the Yard. I had left instructions for a nationwide look out for your Ralph and they had received a telegram from the Lakc District, Keswick, I think, saying that a man of Ralph's description had been seen wandering around the hills in that area. The only trouble is they say he's some kind of 'Bible puncher' or preacher."

Helen couldn't believe her ears.

"Oh my God," she gasped.

"It must be him, it must be him!" she cried, as tears filled her eyes. "That's just what he was like when I last saw him."

"Now, I don't want you to build up your hopes too high, Helen," said the Inspector, trying to calm her down. "I've arranged for this man to be taken to a sanatorium near to Lancaster where he can be looked after."

"Isn't that strange?" she asked, with tears rolling down her cheeks. "That's where it all started, in a sanatorium."

They made arrangements to travel up north together. Ralph's car was the ideal thing to use. Helen thought that seeing it might jog his memory.

As they drove through the large entrance of Lingfield Hospital with its huge iron gates Helen had a feeling of foreboding. She realised that the place was a lunatic asylum and she pressed her hand over her lips tightly, as the tears welled up in her eyes. For her this was going to be the most traumatic emotional experience of her life. She had seen men die with terrible wounds, young boys gassed and blinded never to see again, men in their prime limbless, but this was different, this was her man, her Ralph, the man she loved and the man she would willingly die for.

The Inspector pulled up outside the reception office and they sat there for a moment.

"Are you all right?" he asked as Helen dabbed her eyes with her handkerchief.

"You know you mustn't judge the case before you have seen all the evidence," he continued. "He might not be as bad as you think."

"Yes, I suppose you're right," she replied, trying to pull herself together. "I'm being silly, my feminine instincts got the better of me, but I'll be all right now."

"Good girl," he said, getting out of the car with difficulty. "Now let us see who this man really is."

They were shown into a large plush office by a strong looking man in a long white coat.

"The doctor won't be long," he said, as he left them seated on a leather couch.

"This is all very impressive!" the Inspector remarked, looking around. "This is just what I could do with at the Yard. Yes, very comfortable indeed!" he carried on, as he felt the texture of the leather.

"I hope he won't be long," Helen said, getting a little fidgety. "I do hate waiting, especially for something like this."

No sooner had she finished speaking when the door burst open and in bounced a jolly-looking woman. She was large in the extreme and her overweight frame wobbled about under a tent-like dress that was far too colourful for a woman of her stature. Her hair was a tousled mess and big brown eyes shone out from a moon-like face. As she smiled she showed a set of slightly prominent teeth.

"Well, well!" she said as she bounced across the floor towards them and held out a huge dumpling of a hand.

"You must be the famous Inspector Sharp from Scotland Yard," she said, shaking the Inspector's hand like a pump handle. "My name is Daisy Philpot, God knows why my parents called me 'Daisy', I'm more like a battleship than a flower!" and she roared with laughter, shaking like a jelly as she did so.

"And you must be Miss Graham," she eventually said when she had calmed down and pulled up a large leather chair in front of them.

"Now then, Inspector," she said. "How can I help you?"

A look of puzzlement came over Helen's face at this remark and she was just about to say something when the Inspector, who was ever-vigilant noticed, and reached out, his hand touching hers.

"I asked for a certain man to be cared for," he said, bringing his great frame to the edge of the couch. "A man who was found wandering in the hills around Keswick. The local police told me that he was here."

"Of course, how remiss of me!" she replied slapping her great fat legs. "Yes, he's here, a nice-looking chap now that he's been cleaned up. He's got a split personality. Part of the time he calls himself Ralph. The other part is completely different, then he becomes a fanatical priest called Father Ross or Cross or something like that. Anyway, it is becoming more noticeable that the Ralph person is becoming stronger each day and I expect that in a week or so he will be completely cured. Did he have a shock or a traumatic experience in the last few weeks?"

Helen and the Inspector looked at each other and it was Helen who spoke first.

"Yes, he did, I'm afraid to say," Helen answered. "I was with him when it happened."

"Was it something religious or supernatural?" the doctor asked her.

"Why, yes!" Helen replied, in surprise. "How did you know?"

"Oh, that's easy!" answered the doctor. "We psychiatrists are like artists, we watch, ask questions and from the bits and pieces we paint a picture of the patient's mind. In that way we can help them to recover their sanity. It's all quite simple really."

"Can I see him?" asked Helen.

"I don't see why not," the Doctor replied. "It might do him some good to know that you're here."

She struggled to her feet, saying "I'll come with you to watch his reaction."

The corridors were long and high in this purpose-built asylum. It was more like a prison than a hospital. Screams and moans could be heard coming from all directions. Two strong-armed warders were seen dragging a patient into a padded cell, he was screaming and frothing at the mouth. Helen turned away in horror and wondered what they had been doing to Ralph. Had he suffered the same treatment?

They seemed to be walking for ages through the labyrinth of corridors but it was noticeable that the screams and disturbances from the patients were getting less frequent. It was pointed out by the doctor that the hospital (as she preferred to call it) was in several sections and the further they walked the less violent the patients became. It was still quite a distance that they had walked and Helen was feeling a lot better.

"We put him in a room by himself," the doctor said, stopping at a door. "We thought it better, seeing that Scotland Yard was involved. I'd like Miss Graham to see him alone if you don't mind, Inspector. I will be watching from a viewing panel that we have in every room and I'll have a man standing by just in case."

With this she led the Inspector into the room next door.

Helen stood looking at the closed door. Her hands were clenched so tight that her finger nails were digging into her palms. Then she closed her eyes and said a prayer. A prayer such as she had never prayed before or would ever pray again in her whole life. When she had finished she reached out a shaking hand and turned the knob.

Ralph was lying in a narrow bed looking at the ceiling and he did not move as the door opened. Helen stood there looking at him. She wanted to rush over and take him in her arms but she knew that she couldn't. A few moments passed by and they seemed like an eternity to her. Still he never moved. Helen went a little closer to the bed. She was trying to fight back her tears when suddenly he turned his head and saw her.

His first reaction was puzzlement, he seemed to recognise her but couldn't place her face. He looked away frowning, as though he was delving into the recesses of his mind trying to drag up from its depths where he had seen or met her before. He turned again and looked at her. Suddenly his eyes lit up and his mouth opened as if to say something but nothing came out.

Helen stood shaking with emotion, tears rolling down her cheeks. She was willing him, urging him from the depths of her soul, to recognise her.

"Oh, God, let him know me!" she cried inwardly. "Please, please, let him know me!"

The frown returned to his face and he turned away, struggling with his memory.

"Hello, darling," Helen suddenly found herself saying. It was the last thing in her mind to come out with. She didn't know what his reaction would be, what if he still didn't know her? What if he rejected her as a stranger? If he did, it would destroy her completely. She could have bitten her tongue out if she could. Oh why did she say it? All these thoughts passed through her mind as she looked at him fighting with his clouded memory. She pulled up a chair and sat by the bed.

Ralph turned and looked at her. There were tears in his eyes as he gripped the bedclothes and twisted them in his frustration.

"I seem to know you very well," he said, near to tears. "Do I, do I, know you?"

"Yes," Helen replied, wiping her tears away with her hand. "Yes, you do know me very well. I've been looking for you everywhere and now that I've found you I'll look after you until you're better."

"What's happened to me?" he asked. "I know some things, like I've been to France fighting and they sent me here to this sanatorium. I know who I am. I can remember everything about the war but I feel I know something else has happened to me -something dramatic, something that's affected my whole life. But I can't remember what it is. You say that you know me very well. Then you must know what has happened to me? You can help me to remember?"

Helen reached out her hand to his and they gripped each other tightly.

"You must not worry about it," Helen said softly. "I'm going to stay with you. I'll help you to remember, because I want you to remember."

"I know it must seem crazy to you," he said. "You knowing me well and everything, but what is your name?"

Helen nearly choked on the lump in her throat. Here she was sitting holding hands with her darling Ralph and he didn't even know her name. She didn't know how much more she could take of this, but her aptitude for nursing won the day and quietly she said.

"Helen! Helen's my name. Helen Graham."

Ralph looked searchingly into her green eyes, trying to find something he could latch on to. His eyes narrowed straining to remember where he had seen her before, but after a while he sank back onto the pillow dejected.

"It's no good," he said despondently. "There's nothing there."

It was just then that the doctor came in bouncing and as breezy as usual.

"Well, now, Mr Grant, how are you today?" she said, clapping her pudding-like hands and going around to the other side of the bed. "How do you like your visitor?"

Ralph didn't even notice her, he just lay looking at the ceiling and after a few moments of tense silence the doctor motioned to Helen to leave. Just as she had reached the door he suddenly jumped up and shouted "I met you on a train, I remember! On a bloody train! We had a meal and you talked all the time. You're ... you're a nurse. It's coming back! I can remember, I can!" and he grabbed hold of Helen and danced around the room.

"Yes!" shouted Helen, laughing and crying at the same time. "How wonderful!"

The doctor was enjoying it just as much as they were, clapping and singing as they danced around.

The door burst open and a man in a white coat came in to see what all the commotion was about. He was followed by Inspector Sharp. Ralph stopped suddenly when he saw the frame of the Inspector and he pointed at him for a while. Everybody went quiet as they watched.

"I know you!" Ralph said, all excited. "You're a detective from Scotland Yard. Your name is Sharp, Inspector Sharp!"

"Yes, you're right!" shouted Helen, giving him a huge kiss. "It's all coming back to you. You can remember, you can! Oh, I'm so happy!"

After a period of hand-shaking and back-slapping the doctor said she thought that he should sleep for a while. She didn't want him to get exhausted, it wouldn't do him any good at this stage.

"It's better to remember things a little at a time, young man," she said, trying to calm him down.

But Ralph was having none of that. He wanted to remember everything at once.

"I've wasted enough time racking my empty mind for answers that weren't there," he stormed. "I want to remember everything now, right now!" He went and stood in the corner, looking out of the window.

Everybody went quiet and looked at each other. The doctor seemed disturbed at his outburst. Ralph, who was still looking out of the window suddenly turned to face them all. He was trembling from head to toe, his eyes were rolling, and a strange glow appeared all around him, lighting up the corner.

"Oh, my God!" the doctor cried and she moved forward towards him.

"No, don't!" shouted Helen. " Leave him alone, keep away from him."

The doctor froze as the glow moved away from Ralph and formed into a figure at the side of him. They could see its face, its clothes, everything about it. It was a man in Puritan dress.

"It's Father Ross!" whispered Helen, transfixed by the apparition before them.

The ghostly figure made a blessing and the sign of the cross over Ralph, then disappeared.

For a moment there was complete silence as they realised that the spectre had gone. Then pandemonium broke loose. Helen and the doctor ran over to Ralph, who seemed to be asleep standing up.

"Get him to the bed," the doctor said as she ushered the warder over. "I've seen everything now," she continued, plugging her stethoscope in her ears and feeling for Ralph's heartbeat under his shirt. After a good examination she looked up saying "It's amazing, he's as fit as a fiddle."

By this time Ralph was snoring loudly and they all began to giggle at the noise he was making.

"Would you believe it?" laughed the doctor. "You wouldn't think he'd just gone through something like that, would you?"

"Can I stay with him?" asked Helen. "I'd like to be here when he awakes."

"That would be a good idea," the Doctor replied. "I'll send you some tea down with the Inspector and you'll be company for each other."

When they had gone and their footsteps had disappeared down the passage, Helen held his hand and had a good cry. Out came all her pent-up emotions but she didn't care, she had her Ralph back, safe and sound.

CHAPTER THIRTEEN

It was now the beginning of May. The past eight weeks had been hell for Ralph, Helen and Inspector Sharp. Someone at the asylum had got in touch with the national press and they had been hounded night and day. Fantastic stories had been printed about a supernatural power that was seen to come out of Ralph. He was deemed to be a holy healer. People flocked to the asylum from all over the country. A tented village was erected in the fields outside and a shrine was set up at the main gate.

Another story was that Ralph had come back from the war a raving lunatic with shell-shock and had been miraculously cured by a vision of the Angel Gabriel. This brought near to a thousand mothers and wives, whose sons and husbands had suffered similar ill-effects in the war, all clamouring for a cure for their loved ones. Pictures of all three were featured on the front pages of nearly every popular daily paper and it was quite obvious that they would have to go into hiding until the hullabaloo died down.

It was arranged by the Inspector that they were whisked away in the early hours of morning just before dawn. They were well on their way to Keswick and the safe haven of Polly and Tom's farm before the tented village was awake and the daily routine of the asylum had begun.

The sun rose on a beautiful May morning as they sped along towards Thirlmere. The morning mist hung low in the valleys and not a breath of wind disturbed the new bright green foliage that adorned the trees. This was the first morsel of peace they had enjoyed for weeks and Helen didn't want to miss it.

"Please stop!" she called to the Inspector, who was driving Ralph's car. "I'd like to get out for a moment or two, just to take in the view."

"That's a good idea," he replied. "I could do with a stretch myself," and without further ado he pulled over onto a grass verge and stopped.

"Isn't that wonderful?" Helen said, walking away from the car with arms outstretched. "Did you ever see such a view?"

"It certainly beats London with all it's fog and soot, not to mention the noise," Ralph called, as he followed her to the edge of a cliff that overlooked the lake far below.

They sat together on a long flat rock while the Inspector was pacing about behind them, breathing in the fresh morning air. The peace, quiet and the tranquillity of the whole scene seemed to soothe away all their worries. It was quite some time before anyone spoke and it was Ralph who broke the silence. It was what he said that had Helen staring at him in surprise, because this was the first time he had spoken about his terrible ordeal. She had assumed that he recalled nothing about it and, assuming that, she had never broached the subject.

"It's a strange world, the twilight zone," he began. "You know who you are but at the same time you're somebody else. In my case, my body was being used by Father Ross's spirit. If I was in danger he took over, just as he did on that fateful night at the Manor. I would have been gone forever if it hadn't have been for him."

Helen didn't know what to say to him, so she took his hand in hers and held it tight.

"At first I thought that I was dead. I seemed to be drifting through endless time and I was certain that I was in Limbo but his voice was always talking to me, telling me not to be afraid. There were times when I could feel pressure all around me, as though another force wanted to get inside me, this was when he took over. It was then that the terrible noises began, screaming, howling, as though there was a great fight going on all about me. I remember that it was after one such bitter attack that we were looking down on his village. We seemed to be suspended in space watching, waiting, for something to happen. Suddenly it started to rain, great black clouds opened up, sending down torrents of water the likes of which I have never seen before nor ever will again."

"People were rushing everywhere as their houses began to crash all about them. They were screaming and crying out for help. Soon there was nothing left but a lake with bodies floating on the top. Men, women, children and all their animals were dead. Then a mist surrounded all the lake, making a barrier from the rest of the countryside. Father Ross was showing me how she had imprisoned and bewitched all the valley and everything in it. They were now the living dead and in her power for ever. His voice cried out to me that she must be stopped and he would show me how. He promised that he would guide me with signs and keep me safe at all times."

"That is incredible," came the Inspector's voice from behind. "And this Father Ross, is he one of these undead or 'living dead' as you call it?"

"Oh, yes!" answered Ralph quietly. "I've seen him several times."

"And they'll be this way until Mary Bamford is finally laid to rest or completely destroyed?" the Inspector said, rubbing the stubble on his chin.

"That's what it amounts to, I'm afraid," replied Ralph, "And it's not only the people in the valley who are involved. It's people like Sittwell and all those who were at that coven initiation ceremony, people who have been in her power for generations or have been killed by her. When she goes to stay with her master the Devil for ever, all these people will find peace."

"I can see that we have a mammoth task on our hands!" the Inspector said, sitting down next to Ralph on the long flat stone. "The best way that I can help is by doing some research. I shall busy myself by digging into all the old records in Keswick Town Hall. The mention of Scotland Yard will get me into anywhere."

Silence reigned once again and Inspector Sharp took out his old pipe and began to fill it with his favourite thick twist. Suddenly there was a sound of dogs barking behind them. Ralph and Helen turned in panic but their fears were groundless. For along the road came a chap dressed like a country squire, duck shooting hat, plus-fours, double barrelled shot-gun tucked under his arm, and he was being followed by three Golden Labradors.

He was very tall and thin, and his bearing was military. Bright blue eyes flashed about in all directions and a waxed moustache twitched as he greeted them.

"Good morning!" he bellowed out as he saw them sitting there. "It's a beautiful morning, isn't it? Taking in the view, what?"

Ralph and the Inspector stood up as the man approached.

"Yes, it certainly is," replied the Inspector. "I see you're off shooting, sir?"

"Always do a spot of shooting first thing, gets the blood going, you know!" the man said. "By the way, the name's Fullerton. I have a place just over the hill there," he said, pointing behind him.

Ralph stared at Fullerton for a few moments and then he stepped forward, holding out his hand.

"Ex-Captain Grant, late of the Scottish Highlanders, General," he said, to the great surprise of Helen and Inspector Sharp.

"Oh, you know me, young fella, do you?" laughed the General. "That's the very reason that I moved up here. Used to live in Kensington. Damned nuisance, couldn't walk out of my own front door without being stopped by somebody or other asking me how their Johnnie was. Scottish Highlanders, eh? Damned fine regiment. Yes, been up here since I retired, beautiful spot, wouldn't move back there for a gold clock, what?" and he roared with laughter.

"I have just expressed the same sentiments," agreed Ralph, looking out over the lake. "But it looks as though the weather is turning sour, there are clouds on the horizon."

"Oh, that's not the weather, old chap," chuckled the General. "No, that's what the locals call 'Bamford's Shroud'. It appears now and then over a small lake. The legend goes that the whole population of the valley was drowned by the water that is now the lake. It is supposed to have been brought down on them by a witch in retribution after she had been burnt at the stake. Load of hogwash if you ask me, what?"

The other three looked at each other but said nothing.

"Are you staying in the district?" asked the General.

"Yes, we're staying with friends near to Keswick," Helen answered before Ralph or the Inspector could stop her.

"Oh in that case," the General carried on, "why don't you come over for a sherry and perhaps a spot of lunch one day? Doesn't matter which. I never go anywhere these days. It would make a nice change for me and the dogs."

"That would be very pleasant," Helen said, feeling sorry for him. "We'll do that one day, won't we, dear?" she said turning to Ralph, but when she saw his face she knew she had said the wrong thing.

"Yes, we'll make a point of it," he answered, trying to be polite.

"Fine," the General called as he started off down the road. "I'll expect you then."

He had hardly gone out of hearing distance when Ralph rounded on Helen.

"What did you want to tell him our business for?" he said, furiously.

"We are supposed to be going into hiding, and the first person you come across you tell him where we are going to stay! That's great, that is!"

Helen was near to tears and she looked at the Inspector for some support.

"It's not all that important," he said, taking her part, "but then we can't be too careful."

"Exactly!" said Ralph, walking towards the car. "But there's one consolation, he didn't seem to recognise any of us. Maybe he doesn't read the newspapers."

"I'm very sorry," Helen said, following him and climbing into the back of the car. "I just didn't think."

"There's no harm been done," the Inspector said, starting up the engine. "I think he's just interested in peace and quiet, and his dogs, of course."

All was forgotten by the time they had reached Polly's. It was hugs and kisses all round, even the Inspector was included, and he seemed to like it. As they were taking their things inside the farmhouse Ralph looked up at the black cloud blanketing the hill across the valley.

"How long has that been there, Polly?" he asked. "I don't remember it being there the last time I was here."

Polly looked uncomfortable and didn't seem to want to answer. Ralph had never seen her like that before and he pressed her more closely.

"Is there something wrong, Polly?" he asked quietly. "Is there something that I should know?"

"Oh, I'm just being silly," she replied, and started to go into the house. But he stopped her by taking hold of her arm, saying "Now, Polly, you can't leave it like that. There is something wrong, I know it. Please tell me, maybe I can help in some way."

She stood for a moment looking at him and then she threw her arms up in the air, saying "Oh, I suppose you'll get to know anyway. Come on, I'll show you something." Then she made her way across the farmyard to the barn.

Ralph followed her as she passed through the barn to a pen at the back. There she stopped and opened a small gate. Once inside the pen she pulled back a large tarpaulin to reveal the decomposing carcasses of her favourite cow and eight sheep. The smell was foul and Ralph turned away, nauseated.

"Oh, my God!" he cried out. "Polly, that's terrible! However did it happen?"

"It all started about the first two weeks in April," she began. "I don't listen to old wives' tales but when that cloud appeared everything started to go wrong. It's not just us, but the whole farming community hereabouts have had something similar happen to them, sheep, cattle, pigs, chickens, horses… But the worst was when young Jack Pollard was found up there on the hill under the cloud near Bamford's Lake. He'd been missing for two weeks and when they found him he was hardly recognisable. He was a strapping lad, always fit and healthy, but when they brought him down, and his mother saw him, she swore that it was witchcraft the curse of the Bamford's had returned. As I say, I don't listen to old wives' tales, but it's too much of a, oh, what's the word…?"

"…coincidence…?" said Ralph, helping her out.

"Yes that's it," she carried on. "I'm a simple God-fearing woman, even if I don't go to church as often as I should, but it makes you think. And then if that wasn't enough to put up with, I see your picture in a newspaper, people talking about the Angel Gabriel and spirits being seen and the like…" and then she looked at him as though it was for the first time. Suddenly she clapped her hands over her mouth and stifled a scream.

"Your face!" she eventually gasped. "The scars on your face, they've all gone! Oh, my God! It's true, it's all true!"

Ralph put his arm around her shoulder as she stared up at his face.

"Now, don't get excited," he said, laughing a little. "Part of it is true but the bit about the angel isn't. What I'm more concerned about is all this," he said, pointing to the tarpaulin. "What does Tom think about it all?"

"Oh, you know what he's like," she answered. "He doesn't say much, thinks more, does Tom, but I'm always frightened when he goes off up into the hills. I've noticed though that he's started to wear a crucifix around his neck and that's not like him, he's not the superstitious type."

"How long has he been out this morning?" Ralph asked her.

"He went out at first light," she replied "And he usually doesn't come home till it's nearly dark."

"Where will he be today?" he asked.

"He's gone over towards Bamford Lake," she cried suddenly, bursting into tears. "Oh, Ralph, I am frightened!" and she clung to him as she sobbed.

"Come on, Polly" he said, trying to console her and leading her back through the barn towards the house. "I'll get the car and go out to see if I can find him. It's still early and maybe he hasn't got too far."

When Inspector Sharp heard of Ralph's expedition he wanted to go along.

"It'll do me good to get out in the fresh air," he said as they sped along. "Can't remember when I last climbed a hill or if I'll be able to, now, with all this bulk to carry about."

They had been driving for about ten minutes when Ralph stopped the car on a rise in the road. He scanned the hillside for life of any kind suddenly he called out: "Pass the binoculars, Inspector, they're in the glove compartment."

He took them in haste and quickly focused them on a certain point on the hillside

"That's a stroke of good luck," he said excitedly. "It's Tom" then he stopped for a moment.

"Hold on, there's something wrong with him, he seems to be staggering about and holding his head."

Without further ado he tossed the binoculars into the back of the car, started up the engine and raced off down the road at break-neck speed.

"What's wrong?" shouted the Inspector, clinging desperately to his seat.

"I don't know, but we'll soon find out," shouted Ralph in reply, turning off the road onto the lower part of the hill. He threw the car into a lower gear as he hit the soft moorland type of terrain, skidding and driving the big car for all it was worth at the hill.

"We'll never make it!" the Inspector shouted as they hit the higher ground. "Watch out for the rocks!" he cried, bouncing a foot into the air.

Suddenly Ralph swung the car around to face downhill and they nearly turned over. He jammed the brakes on and threw it into reverse, before switching off the engine and jumping out. He was off like a mountain goat, clambering up the hillside towards the figure of Tom who by now was lying on the ground. The Inspector had only just managed to get out of the car and was making very slow headway up the steep hillside.

Tom was lying at the base of a cliff that ran along the full length of the top of the hill. It rose straight up into the darkening sky, measuring a good hundred feet or more, giving the impression of a medieval fortification and defying anyone to scale its impregnable jagged face to find the secret of Bamford's Lake.

As Ralph reached him and bent over him to establish the extent of his injuries, a great clap of thunder rent the air above them. He looked up to see the black cloud swirling out over the cliff face. With the cloud came a sudden strong gust of wind that whipped up dust and gravel from the base of the cliff into a whirlwind-like cone that came at the pair, stinging, slashing, cutting and blinding them. Ralph tried to drag Tom away but the whirlwind followed them down the slope, making escape impossible. Ralph threw his body over Tom to protect him from the razor-sharp stones. Then just as suddenly as it had started, it stopped. He looked up in amazement, this was his chance to get Tom to safety.

He bent down and tried to lift him to his shoulder. As he was doing this he noticed that there was complete and utter silence all around him. The stillness was uncanny and frightening in the extreme, there seemed to be a presence of evil in the atmosphere. Then, without warning, a gigantic clap of thunder split the silence asunder. Flashes of forked lightning struck the ground all around him, setting the grass on fire. A gale-force wind sprang up from nowhere, whipping the flames into a more ferocious blaze. Ralph dragged the lifeless Tom away from the fire and smoke. He managed to get him half way down the hill to where the Inspector was standing gasping for breath.

"My God, I've never seen anything like it in my whole life!" he shouted to Ralph. "Where did it all come from?"

"It's all her doing!" shouted Ralph in reply. "Come on, we've got to get away from here."

The Inspector grabbed hold of Tom's legs and they had just started towards the car when another ear-splitting clap of thunder filled the air. They stopped for a second to look around, only to see a thunderbolt strike the face of the cliff. They watched in horror as the cliff face seemed to come alive, lifting itself into the air. Suddenly there was a mighty roar as a huge spout of water ripped through the lake's fortification, cascading tons of rocks in its wake. Before they knew it they were being swept along by an almighty flood. Bamford Lake was emptying into the valley below.

The car and all three men were tossed about like matchsticks as the water rushed down towards the road. Luckily the valley veered to the right and the tempestuous torrents rampaged down the natural contour of the terrain, smashing all before it. Nothing stood a chance. Sheep that were grazing on the lower slopes were picked up like fluffy toys and swept along. Trees were uprooted and joined the mass of mud and boulders that were mixed in the powerful rushing waters.

Ralph was being tossed about in the raging waters when suddenly he was smashed up against a stationary rock. He was winded, but he clung on for dear life as rocks and logs crashed all about him. It seemed ages but it was only minutes before the waters calmed and became a gentle flow. As they subsided and carried on flowing down the valley, they left a trail of mud, rocks and destruction.

"Hello! Hello!" came a call from up on the hill to his left. "Are you all right, Ralph?"

Ralph lifted his head for the first time and looked about him. It was Inspector Sharp, and he was sliding down the slope towards him.

"God, I thought you were a goner!" he called, wading through the mud to reach him and help him up.

"The whole lot has emptied itself into a deep gorge. I was lucky, it washed me to the side and I scrambled to safety up the hill. I saw the whole thing. It was horrific!"

"Where's Tom? Have you seen him?" gasped Ralph, trying to get his breath back as they reached a grassy part of the hill.

"I don't think he made it, old chap," the Inspector replied. "I saw his body being swept towards the gorge. I think he's gone."

"Oh, God, poor Tom!" Ralph cried in despair. "And poor Polly too, how the hell am I going to tell her? It's all my bloody fault. If I hadn't come here it would never have happened. Oh, God, what am I going to do?"

"It's no good getting yourself in that state," said Inspector Sharp. "You've been through worse than this in the War. This battle we've lost, but as long as we win the last one, that's what counts."

Ralph dropped his head into his hands. "When is it all going to end? That's what I want to know, how the hell are we going to get rid of her?"

"Come on," said the Inspector, taking charge and pulling him up onto his feet. "It's no good stopping here. Tom's gone and there's nothing we can do about it. We had better get back to the farm and break the bad news to Polly."

They trudged along the side of the hill, keeping well clear of the slowly sliding mud that was making its way towards the gorge, when the Inspector suddenly called out.

"Hell's bells, Ralph, just look at that gaping hole in the cliff face."

Ralph looked across the valley and couldn't believe his eyes. "The whole lake must have emptied!" he called to the Inspector, who by this time had moved further along. "The village must be visible. I'd love to see it."

"You can't go over there in your state, lad," called back Inspector Sharp. "You'll catch pneumonia if you don't get those clothes off sharpish. We'll have a good look tomorrow when it's all subsided."

"I suppose you're right," mumbled Ralph, dragging his wet aching body after him.

They arrived back at the farm just before noon. Polly and Helen were devastated by their news and after a good cry, mixed with a great deal of consoling by Helen, Polly turned to Ralph and took him by the hand.

"You mustn't go blaming yourself for what's happened. Tom is not the first brother I've lost up there. That cursed place has claimed two more. First there was Albert, he was eleven. Died without ever regaining his senses. Didn't know where he was or who he was, and kept on raving about a woman in a white dress until he died. Then there was John, he was older, sixteen. He was a good-looking lad. It broke my mother's heart when he died. He was lost for three weeks. We combed the countryside looking for him and then one day we found him, he was like a skeleton and raving mad. The doctor said it was exposure because he had been lost in the depths of winter, but we knew different. We never said anything to anyone but we knew..."

"Why didn't you tell me all this before, Polly?" Ralph asked.

"Listen, my lad," she replied softly, wiping a tear away. "When Tom found you up there and brought you here to me, we knew what was wrong with you. Never mind what that doctor said. You lay here for days rambling on about a priest and a woman in white just like our Albert did and no-one was happier than me when you recovered. I knew then that whatever it was up there could be beaten. Tom had to go up there, he had to try. There was nothing else he could do, poor soul."

Helen threw her arms around Polly and burst into tears. "Oh Polly!" she cried, "and we thought that we had been hard done to."

"Come on now, Helen," Polly said, consoling her in return. "The people around these parts can tell some sordid stories that have happened over the last three hundred years. People from outside have called us superstitious country folk and we have been laughed at, but, you see, we have been right all along."

"Superstition, legends, witchcraft, call it what you like," said the Inspector, "I know what I've seen with my own eyes. I know that I was sceptical at first bodies torn apart and heads missing, a body that went through a window and disappeared, leaving its clothes hanging on the railings. I am an Inspector of police at Scotland Yard and as such I only investigate facts, logical things that can be scientifically proved, yet this defies all logic. But starting tomorrow I shall combine the two. I shall be at the records department of the Town Hall as soon as they open."

"And I shall be looking at what is left of Bamford's Lake," thought Ralph.

CHAPTER FOURTEEN

The dawn chorus had barely finished when the early light pushed away the remnants of the night. Ralph and Inspector Sharp had been up and about for a good hour. Polly, like all hardened farming stock, had already done half a day's work by city standards. She could be heard busying herself in the kitchen. The sizzling sound of bacon and its wonderful aroma filled the house. Helen was still tucked up in her cosy bed oblivious of the industry and the schemes that were being hatched out below her.

Ralph had decided to go with the Inspector to Keswick. A look at the local records on witchcraft wouldn't come amiss and besides that, he needed to replenish his stocks of holy water as an expedition to the now drained Bamford Lake couldn't be accomplished without it.

"I don't want to sound ungrateful," he said looking through the window at the dispersing morning mist, "but I do wish Polly would hurry. It's a hell of a trek to Keswick and I want to get an early start."

"I hope you're not going to rush me, young Ralph," the Inspector replied. "I'm not used to walking. How far is it, ten, fifteen miles? Don't forget, young fella, I'm used to riding about in cars. All this fresh air and walking could kill me if I'm not careful!" and he stretched his neck high into the air, taking a good sniff as he did so.

"Oh, just smell that," he carried on. "Believe you me, lad, I'm going nowhere until I've got some of that inside me."

The Inspector was as good as his word and it was another hour before they planted their feet on the road to Keswick. Ralph by this time was fuming and he set a cracking pace that left the Inspector a long way behind. After they had covered about five miles, Ralph had lost sight of his bulky friend.

He stopped by the roadside for a while waiting, when a car approached him coming the other way. When the driver saw Ralph he slowed down and stopped. The car door opened and a policeman got out.

"You're out early, sir," the constable said coming over to him. "Everything all right, is it?"

“Yes, everything’s fine now that you’re here, constable,” Ralph replied with a grin.

“I don’t understand, sir,” answered the constable, who was at the retiring age and a little overweight for chasing villains.

“Well, if we drive down the road a bit we will find Inspector Sharp of Scotland Yard trudging along this way and he’ll be very glad to see you,” laughed Ralph.

“Inspector Sharp?” replied the constable in amazement. “Why I was just on my way to fetch him to the station. We knew he was up at the Riddley place,” he said, getting into the car alongside Ralph, “and when Bamford Lake burst we thought we’d better see if everything was all right. Besides there are a few messages from London waiting for him.”

“Has anyone been up to the lake?” asked Ralph.

“Someone’s going up there today,” replied the constable, driving away. “It’s not a place that’s frequented a lot in these parts and we don’t quite know what to expect. It has a bad reputation you know, strange goings-on over the years. There have been five deaths in my time and many more before that, I can tell you.”

“Well, you can add another one to the list,” Ralph said, gravely. “When the lake burst it carried off Tom Riddley, We think he’s at the bottom of the gorge.”

“Oh, that’s terrible,” said the shocked constable. “Poor Polly! How’s she taken it?”

“As well as can be expected,” answered Ralph, “after losing three of her family up near the lake.”

“I didn’t know that” cried the shocked constable, just as he spotted the sweating bulky figure of Inspector Sharp rounding a bend in the road. “There he is!” he called out as he drew the car to a stop beside him.

The constable blurted out all kinds of messages to the Inspector but he just gasped and nodded as he clambered onto the back seat of the car. Then with a loud sigh he said: “Thank God for that! I know I would never had made it all the way to Keswick except in an ambulance.”

The constable laughed and called out to him “We’re not built for walking, sir, especially up and down hills.”

The Inspector nodded again in reply and it was quite a while before he had regained his composure.

"They are going to have a look at Bamford's Lake today," Ralph called out to him after a decent length of time had elapsed. "I'd like to go with them, what do you think?"

"There's no need to go with them," came the reply from the Inspector. "My car's at Keswick, the lads brought it up from the asylum, we can go when we like and take our time about it."

It was quite obvious that the Inspector didn't want to talk, and peace was the order of the day until they reached Keswick police station. It didn't take him long to dispatch a few phone calls to London and as they walked along the main street towards the Town Hall he was still making notes in a little red book that he always carried with him.

"Somebody is keeping the ball rolling at the asylum," he said to Ralph eventually. "Some idiot has seen the Virgin Mary all dressed in white, floating about the grounds."

"Might not be such an idiot," replied Ralph. "How do they know it was the Virgin Mary? It could have been Mary Bamford."

"Hmm, I never thought of that," the Inspector said, grumpily.

From the Town Hall they were sent to the local library. There they were shown into a room that held all the historical documents of the area. There wasn't a great deal on witches and witchcraft. On the subject of the village being flooded, the local documents of the day, which were written by a priest, said it was an act of God and the only mention of the Lady Mary Bamford was that a high-born lady had disappeared in a fire and that it was believed to be her. All her estates, property, rents and so on had passed down to her daughter. This daughter had left the district and gone to live near Aylesbury.

"Seems fishy to me," said Ralph as they walked back to the police station. "I didn't know she had a daughter. And another thing, it looks like a cover-up by the priest, as though they didn't want anyone finding out about the evil goings-on in and around the area, especially while it involved the nobility."

"You could be right," the Inspector replied. "He's been 'got at' by her friends in high places because they would be implicated and might suffer the same fate."

"Exactly!" Ralph mumbled deep in thought. "You don't think that the daughter and Mary Bamford are one and the same do you?"

"Anything could be a possibility," the Inspector replied, then he stopped and looked at Ralph. "You're not suggesting…" then he shook his head and walked a little further before stopping again to look at Ralph.

"What?" asked Ralph, "Suggesting what?" .

"Well," the Inspector started, but shook his head again, saying: "It's crazy, but you're not saying that Mary Bamford has lived at the Manor for three hundred years and it was the same Mary Bamford, the one that was burnt at the stake, that you spoke to at that party on New Year's Eve?"

"Well you said it, not me," answered Ralph. "Anything's possible, you said, and after what's happened to me over the past few months, and after what you've seen with your own eyes, how can you doubt it?"

"Hmm," the Inspector mumbled as they walked into the police station.

"A ghost or a spirit is one thing but speaking to a thing that you can touch is another. God dammit, man, the people in that area know her!"

"Well, where has she disappeared to?" asked Ralph, getting agitated. "Tell me that. Has there ever been a death in that family, or children? Why is it that the present Lady Bamford looks just like the original and why couldn't the police find anything in the ruins of the old Manor House? Surely if she had been a real live woman, and lived as everyone thought that she did in the place, there would have been something left in the rubble, but there was nothing, nothing at all. There has been a nationwide search for her but she has disappeared from the face of the earth.

"There's another thing," he carried on. "Don't you find it strange that all the animal deaths up here started just after her disappearance from the Manor and that black cloud called Bamford's Shroud appeared at the same time? It all fits together, she's here, she's come home because she has nowhere else to go."

By this time they had reached a little office that had been set aside for the Inspector, and the big man sat down at his desk looking at Ralph. As was his nature he took some time thinking about what Ralph had said and after what seemed an agonising pause, he spoke.

"So you think that she is waiting for you up there somewhere in that valley?" he said. "Waiting for the last battle between you and her."

"Don't forget Father Ross," Ralph said. "He'll be there."

"And there's someone else as well that you've forgotten," the Inspector said, flicking through his red notebook.

"You mean Helen?" answered Ralph with a grin, knowing full well who the Inspector was talking about.

"No, me, you fool!" the Inspector shouted at him. "You don't think that I've come as far as this just to sit at a desk and wait for the news, do you? God, I wouldn't sleep at nights if I wasn't in at the kill. I want to know in my heart that all this business of witches and witchcraft is over and done with, and will never raise its ugly head again, ever."

"Well, in that case," Ralph said, sitting opposite the Inspector, "there are one or two things that you ought to know about the supernatural. Firstly, never believe what you see, things can change in a flash, in the blink of an eye. This woman will set out to trick and deceive. She can put you in situations that you wouldn't believe. Forget about detective work, it counts for nothing when you go up against her. What you need is a crucifix and a flask of holy water. These are the only safeguards you can have against the might of this she-devil. Believe me, Inspector, you've seen nothing until you've seen the power of Mary Bamford at work."

"Well, you know I'm not a religious man," the Inspector replied. "But I'll go along with it. It seems to have stood you in good stead and brought you through. There must be something in it."

"Right, let's get cracking," Ralph said, standing up. "I saw an old church on the edge of town and I was thinking it was just the place to get our holy water. Maybe a blessing for ourselves wouldn't come amiss, either."

"Hmm," the Inspector mumbled, not sure what he was getting into.

"Well, if it's got to be this way, it's got to be," he said, pulling his large frame out of the small chair with a grunt. "There's no point in wasting time, let's get on with it."

Ralph was right about the church, it was very old. Some of the gravestones in the churchyard were dated before 1600. What struck him more than anything was the fact that the little church could have been a replica of the church in the valley, and as he walked up to the main door he half expected Father Ross to come out and greet him. The feeling was even stronger as they entered. The Inspector took off his bowler hat and stood looking around as though he didn't know what to do. Ralph on the other hand walked slowly down the centre aisle amazed at the resemblance to the church of Father Ross. The main difference was a stained glass window behind the altar. The church in the valley had a plain wall with a cross on it.

As Ralph reached the altar steps an old priest came out of a side room. He was bent double with age and carried a heavy walking stick to help him along. His hair was as white as snow. The robes he wore were worst for wear and looked dusty, but his voice echoed around the little church as he said to Ralph: "Can I help you, my son?"

Ralph hadn't seen him and was taken aback.

"Oh, good afternoon, Father," he said. "I came to see if you could let me have some holy water?"

"You have a holy rite to perform, my son?" the priest asked, coming closer to Ralph.

"It is for the destruction of evil, Father," Ralph answered, bending and trying to see the old priest's face. "Also for the protection of my friend and myself in the event of a confrontation with the evil force that we have to destroy."

"Holy water is not enough on its own, my son," the priest said. "Do you possess a blessed crucifix? You must have the two to do battle with the Devil."

Ralph took the crucifix that Father Ross had given to him from around his neck and showed it to the old priest. He held it in his hand and pushed it below the unseen face of the bent old man. As soon as he laid his eyes on it the priest gave out a cry and staggered back.

"Are you all right, Father?" asked Ralph, moving forward to assist him.

"I have been waiting for you for a long time, my son," the priest said, his voice shaking with emotion. "And I know what you have to do. Your task is formidable and I shall pray for your deliverance. Bring your friend forward that I may give you God's blessing."

Inspector Sharp, who had been standing nearby, came forward and stood at Ralph's side. The old priest motioned to them to kneel in front of him. As the two men took their positions, the heavy stick the priest was carrying fell onto the floor and a hand was placed on either head. There was silence for a few moments, then the old priest spoke out in a loud voice, quoting from Psalm 97:

"Let those who love the Lord hate Evil
for he guards the lives of his faithful ones
and delivers them from the hand of the wicked.
Light is shed upon the righteous,
and joy on the upright in heart.
Rejoice in the Lord, you who are righteous
and praise his Holy name.

Give thy blessing, O God to these thy warriors
protect them with thy sword and shield.
Bring victory to them and peace to this troubled land, Amen."

There was an eerie silence. Ralph and the Inspector glanced at each other as they knelt down. They fully expected the priest to say something else but nothing was forthcoming. They glanced at each other again and then Ralph looked up.

"He's gone!" he said in amazement. "But how could he? A cripple like that can't just disappear without making a noise of some description. Look there, near the altar," he said, standing up. "Two stone bottles, it must be the holy water."

"Get it and let's get out of here!" the Inspector said, walking off down the aisle to the main door. "It gives me the creeps a fella's there one minute and gone the next, fair makes your blood run cold, it does," he mumbled to himself.

As they went out into the sunlight they were met by a young priest walking between the gravestones. He was singing as he came towards them and when he saw them he stopped and frowned.

"Good afternoon, gentlemen," he said. "Is there anything I can do for you?"

The two men looked at each other like two schoolboys caught in some naughty act, but it was Ralph who spoke up.

"Er, no thank you, Father," he said, a little unsure of himself. "The old priest has seen to us. We wanted some holy water and he gave us this," he said, holding up the stone bottles.

The young priest looked puzzled and replied "Old priest? What old priest? I am the only priest at St Paul's."

The Inspector coughed, giving Ralph the indication that it was time to leave.

"What was he like, this priest?" asked the young Father, looking more puzzled than ever.

"He was old and bent, just leave it like that," said the Inspector, walking past the young priest.

"Old and bent, you say, and did he carry a stick?" the young priest asked with a twinkle in his blue eyes.

"Why, yes," replied Ralph, a little curious at the priest's amusement. "Why, is there something wrong with that?"

"For your information, gentlemen," the priest began, "the old priest you say gave you that holy water has been dead these past three hundred years or more. Come with me and I'll show you something," and he walked off down a path that led amongst the graves to the back of the little church.

"There," he said, as Ralph and Inspector Sharp came up behind him. "There's the poor man's resting place and see, the mason has carved a stick on his tombstone. He was a famous priest hereabouts in the time of the Civil War. He was noted for casting out witches. He had a well known counterpart from..." then he stopped and said "That's funny, his counterpart, a priest called Father Ross, came from the village that has just seen the light of day after nearly three hundred years of being under water, and they say it was a witch that did that."

"Exactly!" said Ralph, as he and the Inspector moved off down the path.

"Wait a minute!" the young priest called to them. "What are you trying to say?"

"Think about it, it'll come to you eventually," called Ralph as they disappeared around the corner of the church.

They lost no time in making a quick getaway and headed for the police station and the Inspector's car.

"That'll keep him guessing for months!" laughed the Inspector as he drove out of town and headed for Bamford's Lake.

"He knew, you know," said Ralph after a long while in deep thought.

"Who?" asked the Inspector.

"The old priest," answered Ralph. "He recognised his old friend's crucifix. He knew that no-one else could have given me that cross but Father Ross himself, and we are the ones he has been waiting for all these years."

"This business gets creepier by the minute," the Inspector said, taking a quick glance at Ralph, "and the sooner it's over the better I'll like it. I can't wait to get back to my dirty office at the Yard and some sane cases like murder and kidnapping or a juicy one like somebody pinching the Crown Jewels."

"They wouldn't come much juicier than that!" laughed Ralph and he warmed to the feeling of friendship that he had found in the large man sitting beside him.

Time passed quickly as the two men chatted and laughed about their experiences together and before they knew it they were driving up to a police road block. The Inspector pulled his window down as a burly constable came up to the car.

"You can't go any further, sir, it's dangerous up ahead," he said, taking a good look at the Inspector and Ralph.

The Inspector pulled some identification out of his inside pocket and showed it to the constable. As soon as he saw it the man jumped to attention.

"We're here to look at what is left of the village," said the Inspector.

"Yes, sir," came the smart reply from the constable and he waved his arm to two of his fellow officers who immediately lifted the barrier.

"Be careful, sir," called the officer. "The road has sunk in places, it could be dangerous to drive too far."

The Inspector waved his hand in answer to the constable's warning and set off slowly down the road. They hadn't gone very far when Ralph put his hand up, saying "That looks a bit rough up ahead. I think we had better get out and walk the rest of the way. I wouldn't like to see you losing your car as well."

"Hmm," the Inspector grunted in his usual way, as he brought the car to a halt.

"Here we go again," he said, struggling to get his fat frame out of his seat. "I won't forget the last time we were here in a hurry."

"Come on," said Ralph picking his way across the uneven surface of the road. "I can't wait to see what's been uncovered. There's a piece of high ground further up, we'll be able to see everything from there," and he went on ahead leaving the Inspector struggling behind.

He breasted the crest of the hill out of breath with the exertion and the feeling of excitement at seeing the valley and the village once again. He wondered if it would be as he remembered it. Reaching out, he supported himself against a solitary tree. A fresh warm breeze blew from below, rustling the leaves above his head. The sun peeped out from behind a cloud and lit up the whole valley.

Ralph held his breath at the panoramic view that was stretched out before him. To the far left, standing on the high ground, was the ruins of the old Manor House. Down in the bottom of the valley was the village in ruins and still partly covered by water. At the end of the village was the little Norman church. It looked to be intact and as the wind gently blew from the valley below he thought he could hear the bell ring.

"Well, what's it like?" came the Inspector's voice from behind him.

"Bloody marvellous!" came Ralph's reply. "I wouldn't have believed it possible. It's just as it was and the church looks all right. God, I can't wait to get down there."

"It's a bit muddy, isn't it?" the Inspector, said coming up to him. "We'll need some waterproof clothing, wellingtons and the like, before we can think of going down there."

"A boat!" said Ralph, without looking at him. "We'll get a boat."

"Somebody's already got one," the Inspector said, pointing over to the village. "It looks like the police."

"Maybe we can borrow it?" Ralph said, excitedly. "Shall we go and see?"

"I don't see why not," Inspector Sharp replied. "But it won't be today, lad. By the time they get back to wherever they've moored it, it'll be too late to do anything."

"First thing tomorrow, then?" Ralph said like an excited schoolboy waiting for a treat.

"I'll make sure of it when we get back to the station," the Inspector replied. Then as he turned to leave, he stopped and looked over towards the ruined Manor.

"That's funny," he said, "is that smoke rising amongst the ruins?"

Ralph looked towards where the Inspector was pointing and a cold shiver ran down his spine.

"No," he answered grimly. "That's not smoke, it's mist."

It was two days before the local police would allow the Inspector to use the boat. He said that it was a bit of local jealousy, because he came from Scotland Yard. They didn't like the big city boys snooping around their patch especially when they didn't know what he was after.

It was just as well, because it took them that long to gather together the equipment that they wanted: thigh boots of the kind fishermen use, oil lamps in case it went dark while they were still in the valley, long poles to feel for solid ground beneath the mud, ropes for various reasons, food for two days just in case of mishaps, two life-belts, matches, a tent and blankets. They left nothing to chance, this was to be the final battle.

The boat had been moored on solid ground just above the village. It meant that they would have to load it and then push it through the mud to reach the water.

"We've got enough stuff here for a trip up the Amazon!" laughed the Inspector as he struck the water with his oars.

Ralph didn't respond to his joke, he was tense and had hardly slept the previous two nights. Every time he closed his eyes he saw Mary Bamford in her long white dress standing amongst the ruins of the Manor. She was laughing and beckoning to him. His stomach was turning over and over as they passed by the tops of ruined houses that stuck up out of the water. The old stone walls were covered in algae. The plants floated around them in the water, mixed with a great deal of weed, making it hard to row. There were no fish in the lake, over the years fishermen had tried to introduce them but with the difficulty of getting to the lake because of the persistent mist, and the strange covering of Bamford's Shroud, somehow the fish didn't survive. The place was deemed to be cursed.

They were making their way towards the church down what used to be the main street of the village. Ralph could just make out what used to be the inn. It was the largest building in the village and he remembered that was where he first met Father Ross. It was as clear to him as though it was yesterday. The frightened little man behind the bar who thought he'd come from the Devil and the driving sleet as he and Father Ross walked towards the church, it was all coming back to him.

"It might be better if we pushed with the poles," called the Inspector, jerking Ralph back to the present. "This weed is making it hard work and I'm not built for that."

"You have a rest for a while," Ralph said, taking up a pole and plunging it amongst the weeds. "We haven't got far to go now. The church is just up ahead. It looks muddy but I think we'll be able to get out and have a look around."

The little Norman church was on higher ground and as they approached the boat slurped to a stop as the water gave way to the mud.

"That's as far as we go!" Ralph called out as he pushed hard on the pole. "We'd better test the ground before we get out."

The Inspector stood up to do just that and the boat rocked violently, nearly throwing them both out. Luckily the movement sent them both clattering to the bottom of the boat.

The two men roared with laughter and the near-disaster took the tension out of Ralph.

"I'll go first," he said, poking about in the mud with the pole.

"It seems firm enough," he said, tentatively pushing a leg through the mud. "But it doesn't half stink."

After two or three attempts Ralph managed to get the Inspector out onto drier land and by now he was wishing that he had come alone, the big man was becoming a handicap. The mud on the higher ground was beginning to harden and it was easier to walk on, so it didn't take them long to reach the little church. Algae had taken over the bottom half of the church tower and what was left of the walls of the main building. The roof had long since collapsed, leaving Ralph wondering what the inside was like.

The tombstones that surrounded the little church were strangely intact, none of them had sunk or toppled over and they seemed to say: "We're still here." Ralph took one last look and headed for the entrance. The oak door that had once been there had fallen from its rusting hinges and rotted down amidst the mud. As he stepped inside a gentle breeze rocked the bell in the tower and he was astounded by a clear note that echoed around the valley as if it was welcoming him home.

The inside of the church was a mess, the collapsing roof had smashed everything. He was looking at rubble, but then he noticed that the wall behind the altar was intact and on that wall was the cross.

"How can that be?" he thought. "Everything else has disintegrated, so it must just be the outside shell. I bet it's rotten," and he was going to leave, when he had the strangest feeling come over him. He couldn't move towards the entrance. Something was holding him back. He tried several times to go forward but to no avail. In desperation he faced the other way looking at the cross, and a voice that seemed to be all around him said "Take it! Take it!"

He felt unsure, it wasn't right to take something from a church, especially this one, something might go drastically wrong if he removed it.

But the voice became even stronger. " Take it for our salvation!" it called to him and he felt himself being dragged towards the cross, clambering, scrambling, falling over rubble. His hands were cut and bleeding as he reached the far wall where the large cross hung. It must have been ten feet tall and a tremendous weight, but he reached up and plucked it from the wall as if it were a feather and in triumph he turned, with the cross held high above his head. He climbed back across the debris that was strewn across the church floor ·

An amazed Inspector Sharp looked on from the entrance. He couldn't believe what he was seeing. There was a glow all around his friend as he carried the cross towards him. The Inspector panicked and ran outside, slipping and sliding towards the boat.

Ralph came out of the little church like a man possessed, crying at the top of his voice:

"Hallelujah, the Lord is with us today! Praise the Lord."

His eyes were wild with excitement as he reached the boat. The Inspector was sitting in the stern, petrified.

"Ralph! Ralph!" he screamed. "Ralph, man, are you all right? For God's sake, Ralph, what's happened to you?"

"The Lord is with us!" Ralph shouted, brandishing the cross and climbing into the boat.

"You can't bring that on board!" shouted the Inspector "It'll sink us."

"Fear not, my friend," cried Ralph, settling himself down in the bows, "we have had a sign and nothing can stop us now."

"But we'll never carry that!" shouted the Inspector, thinking that Ralph had gone mad or was possessed again by the spirit of Father Ross, but all his fears were groundless as Ralph calmly stood up and started to push the boat out into the weed-strewn water.

"Don't worry yourself, Inspector," Ralph called. "I'm all right. As soon we get into deeper water I'll put a rope around it and float it across."

"Across where?" called the Inspector, still a little worried. "Where are we taking it?"

"We're going to erect it amongst the ruins of the old Manor House," replied Ralph, laughing. "She won't like that, I can tell you. If anything can stir her up, that will."

"You're going to provoke her?" said the amazed Inspector. "Won't that be dangerous?"

"That's the whole idea!" replied Ralph as he lowered the cross into the water and lashed it to the boat with a stout rope. "If she gets mad she might get careless and that will give us an edge. Believe me, Inspector, we will need all the help we can get."

"You can say that again by the sounds of it," the Inspector called out. He gave the pole he was holding a mighty shove and at the same time gave Ralph a very strange look.

It took them a good two hours to push to the other side of the valley. Towing the cross made it hard work, it kept getting tangled up in the weeds and they then had to stop to cut it free. The final fifty yards was even worse, they had to get out of the boat and in waist deep mud drag it to solid ground. There in near exhaustion they rested.

"I hope it's going to be worth all this effort," the Inspector said, gasping for breath. "I'd hate to think that we'd done all this for nothing."

Ralph did not answer. He was looking up towards the ruins of the old Manor. Everything seemed different on this side of the valley. The mud was black and slimy and it seemed to cover everything in sight. There were no plants growing over the blackish grey stones as there were on the church. The whole place looked evil and the stench that arose from the slime was the smell of evil. There was a sense of foreboding everywhere.

"Well, it's no good sitting here looking at it," Ralph said, pulling on the rope that was attached to the large cross. "Give me a hand, Inspector. We'll start by erecting this, that should start the ball rolling."

The Inspector took a grip on the rope, and slipping and sliding they managed to drag the cross to a high point just in front of the ruined Manor. Then digging a hole about eighteen inches deep, with knives, they stood the cross upright, but it didn't seem too secure.

"Stones, that's what we want!" Ralph said, looking about. "Some heavy stones around the base for support," and he went over to a pile of slime-sodden stones and picked one up with great difficulty. By the time they had collected enough and placed them all around the cross, the two men were covered in black slime. Ralph went down through the mud to the water to wash the slime away but it wouldn't come off and, what was worse, it was eating into his skin.

"My God!" he shouted to the Inspector "This stuff's alive, it's eating me."

The Inspector stood looking at his hands in horror and he tried to wipe the slime away with his coat sleeve. "What are we going to do?" he shouted in terror. "It's burning like acid."

Ralph, who was standing near the boat, grabbed the rucksack that held the bottles of holy water. He quickly took one bottle out and opening it he poured a little over his hands. There was an instant effect for the slime cracked and fell away as dust, leaving his skin undamaged.

"Here's the answer!" he shouted, holding up the bottle and making his way up to the Inspector who hastily poured some over his hands.

"Be careful not to waste it," said Ralph, turning to look at the cross.

But the sight that met his gaze made his blood run cold. There was a cloud of mist rising from around the base of the cross.

"Look at that!" he cried out, pointing at the cross.

The Inspector, who was facing the other way, turned in panic not knowing what to expect.

"What's the matter?" he called out and nearly stumbled into the slime. "What's wrong?"

"Look at the cross!" cried Ralph in terror. "The mist is rising from the cross!"

Inspector Sharp shifted his heavy frame nearer to the phenomenon and stood looking at it.

"That's heat, that is, lad. Look at the stones, the slime is drying up."

Ralph couldn't believe it but it was true. The stones were drying out fast, so fast that the ground around them started to steam.

"It must be coming from the cross," Ralph said, getting nearer. "It's cleansing the whole place as the heat spreads. It's fantastic."

Within ten minutes they were standing in dust. An area of twenty square yards had dried up and it was still spreading.

"We'll be able to get inside the ruins in no time at all at this rate," Ralph laughed. "It's a miracle. I was told to bring it, you know, there was a voice in the church, it was all around me, urging me on," and he started to giggle and laugh hysterically as he pointed at the cross.

Inspector Sharp lost no time. He strode up to Ralph and slapped him across the face.

"Get a grip on yourself, man!" he shouted at him. "Don't go to pieces on me, not now, not here of all places," and he shook him violently until Ralph suddenly realised what was happening.

"Oh, my God!" he cried out. "What's wrong with me, why did I do that?"

"It's this damned place," the Inspector said, trying to calm him down.

"The whole place is filled with evil down to the very last stone. Anything can happen. Remember what you told me, don't believe what you see or hear. Well, it's happening already. First the slime, then the cross, and now you. We'll have to be careful of everything from now on."

"Yes, you're right," Ralph said as he took deep breaths in an effort to calm his body down. "I knew it would be dangerous but to be hit by this so soon, it makes you wonder what else she has in store for us."

"Well, we won't find out standing here," the Inspector said, going to the boat and picking up an oil lamp.

"I think it's time we had a look inside that place," he said, nodding towards the ruins. "I'm all set. I have my crucifix and my holy water. Now all I want is you."

He took Ralph by the arm and set off up the hill.

The bottom half of the old Manor was still standing, together with part of a tower. There were blocks of stone everywhere and they were all covered with black slime. The stench was overpowering.

"Oh that smell!" said Ralph, as they climbed over the debris to get inside the ruins. "God, it's enough to make you sick."

"It's just like a few dives I know in Town," laughed the Inspector, trying to keep a brave face. "Or a sewer that I know well under Billingsgate, now there's a smell for you!"

The small talk was keeping their spirits up as they looked around what was left of the once-proud Manor House.

"There doesn't seem to be a lot here does there?" the Inspector said, poking about in a dark corner. "What exactly were you expecting to find, Ralph?"

"This is where it all started," replied Ralph, making a move to a doorway at the base of the tower. The Inspector followed him.

"Everything points to here, this is where she finds sanctuary when things go wrong and when things quieten down she starts her evil doings all over again. There must be something here, something that's important to her survival on earth."

"That's all very well," the Inspector replied. "But what is it? We could be looking for months, especially when we don't know what were looking for," and he lit the oil lamp and held it inside the doorway to the tower.

"There are steps going down here," he called out and as his voice echoed around the tower a scuttering noise could be heard coming from below.

"What the hell's that?" he said, looking at Ralph. "There's something down there."

They looked at each other, their eyes getting wider as the noise became louder. Nearer and nearer it came, like the sound of a million scratching feet.

Suddenly a moving black mass appeared on the descending steps and it was coming towards them.

"Rats, bloody rats!" cried the Inspector. "Oh, my God, there are thousands of 'em!" and he turned, running frightened for his life,

Ralph, who had seen enough rats to last him a lifetime in the trenches on the Somme, threw himself against the wall close to the doorway as the rats spewed out and covered the ruins. The Inspector had fled in panic and had found refuge on what was left of the grand fireplace in the main hall. The rats were everywhere, there seemed to be thousands of them, all squealing and squeaking. They didn't seem to be going anywhere, they were just running around in circles as though they too were frightened. After a while Ralph, who by now had recovered from the initial shock, noticed this unusual behaviour. He could hear the Inspector screaming and shouting at the rats in the old main hall. Another thing he noticed was that the rats were still coming up the stairs from under the tower.

"This can't be," he thought. "There can't be that many rats in the whole of Cumberland. This is one of her tricks to keep us from going down those steps. There must be something down there, something that's very important to her, maybe the very thing we're looking for," and he looked again at the continuous stream of rodents. As he did so he felt the bottle of holy water in his pocket and wondered. Without more ado, he took out the bottle and sprinkled some of the water across the door opening. The effect was amazing. Suddenly all the rats disappeared.

"I knew it!" he cried out. "It was an illusion," and he went in triumph to find the Inspector. He found him standing on top of the highest point of the derelict fireplace still looking around for the rats. When he saw Ralph he couldn't believe it.

"Where have they gone to?" he called to him, still looking all around. "Where are they, the dirty bastards, where have they gone?" It was his turn to be nearly hysterical, for rats were the one thing he couldn't stand.

"They've gone," Ralph said smugly. "They were an illusion, just an illusion."

"Don't be bloody stupid, man," the Inspector shouted at him, his huge body shivering in disgust. "How could they be an illusion? I could feel them running over my feet and I could hear them. God, it was bloody awful."

"Well, they were," Ralph said, clambering over to where his friend stood on his high refuge. "The holy water got rid of them. I just sprinkled some across the doorway to the tower and they all disappeared, just like that," he said, snapping his fingers.

"You sound just like a damned magician on the stage," the Inspector replied, feeling very embarrassed and ashamed at letting Ralph see him in such a state. "Just like that, eh!" he said, climbing down but still looking for any signs of the rats.

"Illusion, eh? Well, what about that, there?" he cried in triumph, pointing at some rat droppings. "What do you call that, Mr Magician, rice pudding?" and he glared wildly at Ralph as he waited for an answer.

Ralph didn't know what to say. The droppings were everywhere and he turned to the Inspector, looking dumbfounded.

"Ha, ha, Mr Magician!" cried the Inspector, rubbing in his advantage. "Cat got your tongue, has it?" and he walked past Ralph mumbling: "Bloody illusion indeed! I know bloody rats when I see 'em."

"I didn't mean to sound conceited," Ralph said, following after him. "It really did work. One minute they were there and the next they were all gone."

"It doesn't matter now," the Inspector replied. "They've gone but they were no illusion, lad."

Ralph felt it best not to press the argument and did not reply. He just went straight over to the tower doorway and stood there looking down the steps into the blackness below.

"What do you think's down there?" came the Inspector's voice from behind him.

"I couldn't hazard a guess," he replied, without looking round. "But I do know this, that whatever it is it's going to be terrible and we're going to need every bit of courage we can muster if we are to come up those steps alive" .

"Hmm, I don't like the sound of that!" the Inspector said, giving Ralph an oil lamp to light. "We had better stick close together, getting separated would make it easier for whatever's down there."

"Good thinking," Ralph replied. "Before we venture down there put your crucifix on the outside of your coat, it acts as a first line of defence, and while we're at it" he said, sprinkling holy water over the Inspector, "a little of this won't do any harm."

"I suppose we need all the help we can get," the Inspector replied, getting himself ready for the unknown.

"Right, I'm ready when you are, lad," he said, giving Ralph a worried look. Then he did something that surprised Ralph greatly, he crossed himself and kissed the crucifix that hung around his neck.

Ralph looked at him and smiled, then he followed suit while the Inspector looked on. When he had finished the Inspector nodded his approval with a grunt and said: "Well, shall we go?"

They descended into the darkness, Ralph leading the way. The steps wound round and round, taking them deeper and deeper underground until at last they came to a passage that had been hollowed out of the solid rock. They slowly followed the passage for fifty yards, then it opened out into a kind of vault. They stood there in amazement, their lamps held high above their heads. The walls were full of recesses and each recess held a body, or what was left of a body.

"My God!" the Inspector gasped. "It's a catacomb, there must be hundreds buried here. Where did they all come from?"

"I thought they only had this sort of thing in Rome," whispered Ralph, walking to the centre of the vault. "I wonder who they are and how they came to be here?"

The Inspector, who was used to corpses, was taking a closer look at them when suddenly he turned to Ralph, holding something in his hand.

"Well, they are not all ancient," he said. "Look at this" and he held out a cap. "This is only about three years old, if that. There's something funny going on here."

Ralph took the cap from him and examined it closely. "Good God, Inspector!" he said. "There's a name tag inside it. Just look who it belonged to!" and he handed it back to him.

The Inspector held the cap close to his light and read aloud "William Sittwell". He looked at Ralph in amazement.

"Well, I'll be damned," he said. "I wonder how many more unfortunate missing people lie in these holes?"

"This is where they'll all be," replied Ralph. "All her victims from over the years. Polly's brothers, the villagers, everyone that crossed her path, their bodies lie here. Good God, it's incredible, unbelievable! She's like some huge spider that's stored them away for a later date."

The Inspector stood there thinking and looking at the closeted bodies. "You said..." he started to say then he stopped and shook his head. "No, it can't be, it's impossible."

"Go on," Ralph pressed him. "I said what?"

"It's crazy," the Inspector carried on, "but you told me that it was Sittwell who was in your room that night, remember?"

"Yes, that's right," Ralph answered. "What of it?"

"Well, if that was Sittwell that night," the Inspector said, looking at the cap, "who the hell is that and how did he rise up and get into your room?"

"He is now one of the living dead," Ralph said, looking him straight in the eyes. "In fact, they are all the living dead, doomed to roam the earth for all eternity. If we win then they will be free to rest in peace."

"Yes, I've heard you speak of this before," replied the Inspector. "But you know it's hard for a policeman like me to believe in such things. It's tangible evidence that I go on, not things that can pass through walls."

"But you've seen them with your own eyes!" protested Ralph and he was just about to embark on a list of previous experiences when the Inspector cut him short.

"What's that over there?" he said, walking over to the other side of the vault. "Look at this," he called out to Ralph. "There's an opening here," and his light disappeared as he ventured inside.

"Wait for me," Ralph called out as he followed him through the opening.

They had entered into a strange circular chamber. It was about forty feet across and twenty feet high. Their lights lit up stone carvings of ravens that stood in niches all around the walls. The rest of the room was bare. The ravens were larger than life, approximately three feet six inches high. Their heads were all looking towards the centre of the floor.

"This is a strange place," the Inspector said, walking around and looking at the statues. "I wonder what went on in here?"

"Yes, I wonder," answered Ralph, feeling very uncomfortable. "I think that we should get out of here, this place smells of evil."

"What were the birds for?" the Inspector said, holding up his light to get a closer look at them. "Do you think they were some kind of guard? They all seem to be looking at the floor, maybe there was something standing there at one time, you know, maybe a tomb or something like that?"

Ralph held his light up looking around at the ravens. The Inspector was right, they were all looking towards the centre of the floor. He went over to the middle of the vault for a closer look. At first he couldn't see anything, the floor appeared to be of solid stone. Then he noticed a line, a thin line, that showed through the drying slime that covered the floor.

"There's something here," he said, scraping the floor with his boot. As he scraped the line became clearer. "There is something," he said. "There's a stone set in the floor, it looks like a tombstone."

The Inspector came over to help with the cleaning and it soon became quite clear that it was a flagstone, three feet long by two feet wide.

"It's not a tomb," the Inspector said. "There's no inscription, maybe it's a cover to something, or somewhere. Another chamber, perhaps?"

"I doubt it," Ralph replied. "We're a long way underground as it is, I can't see there being another chamber below this. Lets try and get it up!"

"We'll never move that," the Inspector replied. "It must weigh a couple of hundredweight. Anyhow we haven't any tools."

"I have a good knife and there's a crowbar in the boat," Ralph said, excitedly. "Here, start scraping and I'll fetch the bar." He thrust the knife into the Inspector's hand and left him standing opened-mouthed in the middle of the vault.

It wasn't long before he was back, brandishing a long crowbar. "This must have been left by your chaps," he said, looking to see how far the Inspector had progressed.

"It won't take long with this," he said jamming the crow bar into the crack.

They worked furiously for an hour, chipping away at the edge of the solid rock that surrounded the flagstone and at the end of their strenuous efforts a small hole appeared below it.

"There is something down there," Ralph said, pushing the crowbar into the hole. "Here," he called to the Inspector, "put your weight on this."

The two men pushed and strained then suddenly the stone began to move, slowly at first, then the Inspector stood on the crowbar, lifting the stone out of the ground. Ralph held on to the stone as the Inspector came to help him push it to one side. Quickly they held their lamps over the exposed hole and looked down. Their lights split the darkness to reveal a hole three feet deep. At the bottom of the hole stood a large silver casket studded with diamonds. The two men looked at each other in amazement.

"Good God!" gasped the Inspector. "Just look at that, we've found treasure!"

Ralph pulled at his bottom lip in thought as he looked down at the casket. "It's not what I expected to find," he said eventually. "I thought it might have been her grave, and we could have finished it here and now, but this has thrown me. I don't know what to think now."

"Let's get it out and see what's inside it," the Inspector said, kneeling beside the hole. "That box alone must be worth a fortune."

"I don't know," replied Ralph. "I have a strange feeling about it."

"A box can't do us any harm," the Inspector said, in a huff.

"It's not the box, it's what's inside it that worries me," Ralph replied, cautiously looking around at the flightless sentinels that were watching their every move. A fearful shiver ran through him as he made contact with their cold staring stone eyes.

"We won't find that out unless we look inside the damned thing, will we?" he heard the Inspector saying. "Come on, help me to lift it out."

Ralph put his lamp down at the side of the hole. He looked down at the casket and then at the Inspector.

"Come on, lad lift it out," he heard him saying, but a voice inside him was crying out to him "Beware, beware!" and his hand was shaking as he reached down to the casket. As they began to lift it towards the top of the hole Ralph's crucifix, which was hanging down in front of him, touched the casket. Suddenly both men let out a cry and dropped the box. As the casket hit the solid rock at the bottom of the hole it burst open and a grey-white dust spilled out.

"What the hell was that?" shouted the Inspector, holding his hand. "It suddenly felt red hot."

Ralph wasn't taking any notice of him. He was staring at the dust in the bottom of the hole. It was beginning to rise into a cloud to the top.

"Get out! Get out!" he shouted in horror at the Inspector, but as he did so he heard a terrifying scream from behind him. He swung round to face the unknown horror and he screamed out in terror as a grotesque huge black raven swooped on them out of the darkness, followed by another and another, all screeching, clawing and pecking, with their eyes burning like fire. Soon the whole vault was filled with beating wings and terrifying screams as the two men fought for their lives.

Ralph saw the Inspector go down under the incessant attacks and it was only then that he thought of the holy water. Punching, kicking and screaming, with his back against the vault wall, he managed to get a grip on the stone bottle. There wasn't time to pull out the cork so he smashed it against the wall and frantically waved the broken bottle in the air, splashing the water everywhere. The effect was dramatic: as the water hit some of the birds they fell to the floor, letting out terrifying screams. When the other birds saw them writhing in agony they stopped attacking the men and pounced on their afflicted allies, tearing and ripping them to pieces.

This was his chance to escape and he dashed over to where the Inspector was lying. He was all crumpled up against the wall. Ralph couldn't see if he was alive or dead and he tried to drag him towards the opening. In a last desperate effort to keep the birds away from them, Ralph threw the stone bottle into the midst of the screaming carrion and more violent screams erupted from within the mass of feathers.

Where Ralph got his strength from at this time he would never know, but he pulled the huge frame of the Inspector into the outer chamber and part-way down the passage to the tower steps. Then he felt a pain in his side. It was like a knife being thrust into his flesh. He stopped for a few seconds, trying to catch his breath, when it happened again. This time it was worse and he let go of the unfortunate Inspector who fell in a heap at his feet.

Ralph grabbed in anguish at the area of the pain and in the pitch blackness he fully expected to feel the wetness of blood flowing from a wound. To his amazement it felt hot and he rummaged in his pocket, feeling for the cause. His heart leapt as his fingers closed around Father Ross's gold crucifix, and as he drew it out it was glowing, giving enough light to see where he was and where he was going. But as he tried to drag the Inspector towards the tower steps the glow became dimmer. Ralph stopped and gently lay the Inspector down. He held the crucifix out in front of him and took a few steps down the tunnel. As he did so the glow became brighter, a few more steps and even more brighter. He stopped and looked back at the Inspector lying there.

"This could only mean one thing," he thought. "I've got to go back. There's something he wants me to do."

With each step the terror in his heart grew. He knew full well the horrors that Mary Bamford could create and he could expect the worst at any time. He reached the catacombs without incident and he crossed over to the vault entrance. The crucifix became brighter. He stopped and listened, everywhere was quiet, so quiet it was frightening and the hairs on his neck began to tingle. The cross seemed to jerk towards the vault, urging him on. Ralph swallowed hard, his throat was bone dry and he was shaking from head to foot as he followed the cross in his extended hand.

The crucifix lit up the vault like daylight. The ravens were all dead and strewn about the floor. He stood there petrified, wondering what he was expected to do, when suddenly a mist started to rise from the hole. He tried to go to the entrance but somehow he couldn't move a muscle: he just stood staring at the ever-growing mist. It rose slowly at first, swaying from side to side, then it suddenly expanded, reaching up to the ceiling. Then in the centre of the mist a face emerged, it was hovering about a foot from the ceiling. It was the face of a very old woman, a hideous face, a face that had known a million sins, wrinkled beyond belief, scaly and hairy. Warts were in abundance and as she opened her mouth she showed a toothless grin.

"So you have found me out, Ralph Grant?" she screamed at him and followed it with a terrible laugh. "You don't remember me like this, do you? Would you have made love with me, seeing me like this?"

She gave another hideous laugh.

"But I will have you again, Ralph Grant, you will be mine forever, along with the rest of them that wait out there in their resting places, just listening for my call."

Ralph's eyes were wide with fear as he stared at her, then suddenly she changed, she was her young beautiful self once more, just as she had appeared to him at the cottage.

"This is what you wanted to see, isn't it, Ralph Grant?" she called in a sultry voice that sent shivers up his spine as he looked at her lovely body. He started to remember the nights at the cottage oh, the ecstasy of those wonderful nights when she would come to him. Oh, the sensual delights that she brought to him! She could be as soft as a kitten and as wild as an alley cat. He was remembering the touch of her wonderful body against his. All the time her voice was soothing and urging him to remember, rekindling a deep feeling inside him that he had suppressed for so long. His mind was filled with her, only her, he wanted her and his arm began to drop, lowering the crucifix. Suddenly he felt a sharp pain that ran through his entire body and it brought him back to his senses.

He realised what she was trying to do and that he had nearly fallen into her trap. With renewed endeavour he held the cross higher.

Seeing this she changed into the old hag, swearing and cursing at him, threatening him with everlasting torment and damnation. She threatened him with the pox, leprosy, syphilis and running ulcers, and said he would beg her to let him die. But still he held the crucifix up high in defiance of all her threats.

Then something happened that he didn't expect. Suddenly Helen appeared at her side and the old hag screamed with laughter at the horror that showed on his face.

"Then you can remember this for the rest of your miserable life!" she screamed at him. "If you won't be mine then you cannot have this wretched specimen you call a woman..." and she struck out at Helen, severing her head from her body. Blood spurted everywhere as he screamed out in horror. He was beside himself with grief and he threw the gold crucifix at the spectre of the old hag, but it dropped short and fell into the hole. There was an instantaneous reaction from the hole and a powerful light burst upwards into the vault. Mary Bamford screamed out in horror, the rock-hard floor of the vault started to tremble, cracks opened up all around. Ralph fled in terror to the opening, the whole place was falling apart. His last sight of her was of flames creeping up her body as she writhed in agony. Suddenly a violent wind sprang up and everything was being sucked down into the hole. The decomposing bodies and skeletons from the catacomb were snatched from their crevices, as mud and slime oozed its way towards the ever-growing hole.

Ralph was fighting for his life against the quickly rising mud. He struggled frantically, gripping the walls of the catacomb as the bodies squelched out all around him. Grinning skulls and fleshless corpses knocked into him on their way down to hell as the Devil claimed his own.

Scratching and clawing his way, Ralph finally reached the tunnel where the wind seemed stronger and after several attempts he managed to get to the tower steps, but there was no sign of the Inspector. The whole place was beginning to disintegrate. It was hopeless looking for the Inspector and he fought his way on hands and knees against the raging wind as he climbed the steps. When he reached the top the whole place was shaking and moving. The once-proud Manor was in its final death throes as the last of the ruins crumbled. But a joyous sight met his eyes, the Inspector was staggering about amidst the mayhem, his arms outstretched, calling for him.

"I'm here! I'm here!" Ralph called, rushing the best he could towards him, but as the Inspector turned Ralph had a horrible shock. There was blood all over his face and as he came closer he realised that the Inspector had lost his eyes to the ravens.

"Help me!" he cried in his pain and terror as he staggered about. "For God's sake, help me! My eyes, I can't see, I can't see..."

Ralph threw his arms around him and tears poured down his face as he gripped his friend.

"Come on, you'll be all right now," he said. "I'll get you away from here. Just hold on to me," and he led him towards the waiting boat.

The ground was trembling violently as he pushed on his pole, trying to get as far away as possible. The Inspector was lying in the bottom of the boat, moaning in agony. Soon they were drifting in the water amongst the weeds and Ralph collapsed exhausted. He had just put his head between his hands in despair when an almighty explosion rent the air. He looked up in horror and saw a gigantic ball of flame and smoke rising from the hillside where the old Manor House had stood. As he watched in terror he saw the smoke and flame suddenly get sucked back into the hole it had made in the hillside, and it was followed by every remaining stone of the old Manor. In a short while nothing was left except a bare mound with the cross from the little church standing alone.

Everything went quiet and once again Ralph dropped his head onto his hands in exhaustion. The boat drifted slowly, rocking the two men peacefully, then a familiar sound stole the peace of the moment. Ralph lifted his head to listen. It was the church bell, quietly at first then joyously ringing out the peal of victory over evil.

He listened for a short time but the thoughts of losing Helen, the Inspector's eyes and the emotional exhaustion of the past few hours, had been too much for him and he passed out.

He awoke in Polly's little bedroom. Helen and Polly were sitting there looking at him. Helen was crying. He opened his mouth to say something but Polly spoke first.

"Seems like you've been in this position before, my lad," she said wiping his brow with a damp cloth. "The police found you and the Inspector in a hell of a state and brought you here. You've been out for two days and we've been worried to death. What were you doing in that valley, anyhow?"

Ralph reached out his hand to Helen, who took it gladly as she wiped away her tears.

"You're all right?" he whispered. "Oh thank God, it must have been an illusion."

"What do you mean?" she asked. "I'm fine, it's you we were worried about. What happened out there?"

"How's the Inspector?" he whispered in a weak voice. "How's he taking it about his eyes?"

"There's nothing wrong with his eyes," answered Polly. "They were all stuck up with blood when the police found you, but he had a bottle of clean water in his jacket pocket so they washed him down with it and it all came off. Fancy being worried about a thing like that, I ask you!"

"He's all right, really," Helen said, leaning over and giving him a kiss. "It's you that we were all worried about. The Inspector has gone back to London on the early train. He's as fit as a fiddle and he said to tell you to hurry up and get better. Oh, and he'll be in touch."

It was two more days before he was fit enough to tell Helen all about what had happened in the valley. The silver casket must have held the remains of Mary Bamford and the gold crucifix was so hot that it set fire to the dust, thus destroying her for ever.

Six months later, Ralph and Helen were married and settled in Chelsea.

It was on a warm sunny Sunday afternoon that they heard a knock at their front door. Ralph went to open it and nearly passed out at the sight of the person standing there. She was tall, blonde and very beautiful.

"Mr Grant?" she said in a low sultry voice. "I believe you knew my father, Major Jack Ryan…"